I don't remember the walk to my car, all I knew is that by the time I got there, I was angry. Very, very angry. I sat alone, gripping the wheel and staring straight ahead. Time stretched out, but I couldn't move. The sun set, and the sky turned orange. It might have been beautiful for all I knew, but at that moment I had no use for sunsets or beauty. I just wanted all the lights to burn out so I could be alone in the dark.

Bridging the Gap

by

Kevin Johnson

This is a work of fiction. Names, characters, places, and incidents are either the product of the author's imagination or are used fictitiously, and any resemblance to actual persons living or dead, business establishments, events, or locales, is entirely coincidental.

Bridging the Gap

Cover Art by *Jennifer Greeff*

The Wild Rose Press, Inc.
PO Box 708
Adams Basin, NY 14410-0708
Visit us at www.thewildrosepress.com

Publishing History
First Vintage Rose Edition, 2020
Trade Paperback ISBN 978-1-5092-3385-4
Digital ISBN 978-1-5092-3386-1

Published in the United States of America

Chapter 1

Wednesday, May 15th, 2002

It was a day like any other day. I hadn't slept well because I was stressed out about work. When the alarm on my bedside table sounded, I had only been asleep a few hours at best.

It was six in the morning and I contemplated, as I was beginning to do more often, just rolling back over and going to sleep. Unfortunately, I needed to pay rent and a long list of other bills, so I rolled out of bed, stumbled my way into the shower and managed to get somewhat clean.

By the time I was dressed and out the door, traffic was already getting heavy. I tried my best not to get enraged at the idiot drivers I had to share the road with, but I failed miserably. When I pulled into the parking lot at St. Edwards Mercy Hospital, I was not in the best of moods.

I clipped my ID badge on and tried to avoid looking anyone in the eye as I made my way to the technology offices. As I entered the main tech area, which was just a large, windowless room filled with cubicles to house much of the IT staff, I saw Amy.

Amy's cube was closest to the door, and because I was usually a few minutes late, I saw her every morning. And, because I usually tried to leave a few minutes early, I saw her almost every evening. She was beautiful. Every nerd in the tech offices practically drooled over her. It was pathetic.

"Good morning," I greeted her.

She looked at me, nodded, then returned her focus to her monitor. She hadn't stopped typing while doing so.

"I like your sweater," I added, feeling especially bold.

She stopped typing as she closed her eyes and sighed. I got a quick sense that something was bothering her. She was obviously having a bad morning and wasn't up for small talk or compliments. I glanced down at the floor, then toward my cube at the back of the room. She opened her eyes and resumed typing, and I walked to my cubicle, feeling much less bold.

As soon as I sat down in my chair, my desk phone rang. It was all I could do to bring myself to answer it. I knew what was waiting for me.

"IT," I said, trying not to sound too put out.

"HERK is down."

I sighed, perhaps a little too loudly. "Okay, I'll check it out."

HERK was the bane of my existence. It stood for Hospital Electronic Records Keeping. A more unoriginal and uninspiring name could not have possibly been dreamed up. The application itself was a gigantic turd most likely written by the same unimaginative people who named it. Although, I did get amusement from the fact that it sounded like a slang term for vomiting.

Anyway, it went down a few times a week. Granted, all I had to do to get it working again was reboot the server on which it resided, but it was the principle of the matter. If the hospital was going to pay thousands of dollars for software, it should at least run more than three days in a row. Of course, some people would blame the server I built, but some people are jerks.

After rebooting the server and calling the records office to let them know I had once again worked miracles, I started combing through the event logs and performing what routine maintenance could be done without any outages. What felt like seventeen hours later, but was only two, I glanced up from my work and saw Amy talking to our boss, Jeff. He said something, and she touched his arm briefly as they both laughed. When they finished what I'm sure was a boring conversation about boring work crap, Amy headed toward the kitchen. It looked like whatever was bothering her earlier that morning was long forgotten, and she was in a much better mood.

My cube was close to the kitchen, although that was a bit of a grand term for it. It was really just a converted office with an ancient refrigerator, a microwave, and a sink, along with two small tables and some mismatched chairs. As she neared, I thought I might try to resume the conversation from earlier.

"Hey, Amy," I said as she was passing by.

She stopped. "Yes?" She seemed to be irritated about something again. It hit me that I may have misread her conversation with Jeff. She was obviously still in a bad mood because of whatever had been bothering her earlier.

"Never mind," I mumbled, looking intently at my monitor. She continued on to the kitchen.

What a trooper, having to put on a happy face for Jeff, who was a complete tool, by the way. And selling it with the touch to the arm was pure genius.

I guess you have to do what you have to do to get by in here.

When lunchtime finally arrived, I walked down to the cafeteria rather than joining my colleagues in our crappy kitchen. They usually avoided the cafeteria like the plague, citing its lousy food and high prices. Luckily, I could choke down just about anything that was thoroughly cooked and, since I was terrible with my finances, the prices were a non-issue. It was also a place I could complain incessantly about the other IT nerds to Sara.

Sara and I had met in college. She was pursuing a Health Science degree while I was working on a Computer Science degree. We met in a math class we were both struggling to pass. We started meeting several evenings each week at the campus library to compare notes and help each other out with the assignments. We struck up a friendship and stayed in touch from that point on. Even after graduating and going our separate ways, we would still talk via phone and email several times a month. She had started work at St. Edwards in Fort Smith soon after graduating, while I spent several years working at an IT firm in Little Rock, where I was completely miserable. One particularly gray winter evening, I was complaining to Sara about how much I hated Little Rock and missed home. Two days later, the phone rang. When I answered, Sara told me about a job opening in the IT department she had seen on the hospital's website. I applied and, two months later, began the move back to

Fort Smith to a new job and a new life. Or something like that. I rented an apartment in the same complex where Sara lived, based on her recommendation that they were nice yet still affordable. And the location was great. Three years later, not much had changed from when I first moved back.

When I walked into the cafeteria, Sara was already sitting at one of the tables next to a large plate-glass window. I waved, and she waved back as I headed to the counter to place my order.

"Hello, Eric. What'll it be today?" Marge asked.

Marge and I were on a first name basis due to the fact that my lunch choice rarely wavered. She seemed to find that fascinating, or maybe just plain weird. Either way, it led to multiple conversations and eventually we were like old friends, making fun of each other's choices in food, fashion, etc.

"The usual," I said.

She poked at the screen in front of her. "One grilled ham and cheese combo. That will be $9.78."

I fished my wallet out of my pocket, dug out a ten-dollar bill, and handed it over.

"Keep the change," I said.

She handed me a Styrofoam cup. "Enjoy."

I nodded, walked over to the soda machine and filled my cup with Dr. Pepper, then joined Sara.

"When are you going to stop drinking that crap?" She nodded toward my cup.

"When the supply runs out," I said as I sat down.

"For your sake, I hope it does soon."

Sara was a bit of a fitness freak. She was always going for runs along the walking trail that ran beside our apartment complex. She had asked me to join her many times and I had said no many times. It was a little game we played.

"So, how are things in IT?" she asked as she tucked a strand of her long brown hair behind her left ear.

"Same old crap. How's life in clinical research?"

She sat up straight. "Good. In fact, there's a new drug trial that has been showing promise in breast cancer patients. Some of the initial studies have shown some optimistic results, so it's a pretty big deal. The research center in Tulsa is taking participant recommendations. We actually have a patient right now that I am going to recommend to Dr. Carver. Hopefully, he'll approve and try to get her in."

I nodded as she began unpacking her lunch.

Without fail, she always brought her lunch and it was always something healthy and disgusting. Things like celery. Gross.

"Did you hear about the layoffs?" she asked as she unwrapped a large chunk of broccoli.

"I did. I'm sure it's like last year. Just rumors. Even if it's true, I should be safe. Without IT, this place wouldn't be able to function."

Sara nodded. "Sure," she said, obviously seeing my point.

"You should be safe, too. Right?" I asked. "Isn't clinical research pretty essential?"

"I hope it is."

"Me, too." A troubling thought struck me. "I hope they don't get rid of Amy."

Sara sighed loudly. It was an annoying habit she had developed. "Are you still stuck on her?"

"What? She's hot," I explained.

"So what? That doesn't make her a good person.

And it certainly doesn't make her the right one for you."

"Oh, I'm pretty sure it does," I argued, only half joking. "Besides, what do you know about it? You're still single, after all."

"My own relationship status has no bearing on whether or not I can see if someone is completely wrong for you."

I watched in horror as she crammed a piece of broccoli into her mouth and began to chew. Luckily, my food arrived just in time to distract me from the terrible act.

"Here you go, hon," Marge said as she slid the tray in front of me. "See you at three?"

"You know it," I replied and dug in.

****

Back at my desk, I more or less focused on work as I bided my time until three o'clock, which was when I took my last break of the day. Without that last break, afternoons would probably be unbearable. Other than the end of the workday, my 3 p.m. break was what kept me going after lunch.

As I watched the time at the bottom right corner of my monitor reach 2:57, Chip's massive head popped up over my cubicle wall just above my monitor, causing me to jump.

"Jesus, Chip. Would you not do that?"

He smiled sheepishly as he pushed his glasses, which had slid down to the end of his nose, back into place. "Did you hear about the layoffs?"

I nodded. "Yes, I heard. I'm sure it's nothing."

Chip was a worrier. He was smart, rational, and methodical when it came to anything computer related.

It's what made him so good at his job managing the hospital's firewalls and handling most of the network security tasks. His mind worked much like a computer in that regard. However, when it came to everything else in the world, Chip was a train wreck. He worried over everything he couldn't control.

"I'm not so sure," he said. "What if it actually happens this time. Aren't you worried?"

I looked up from my screen. "What? Why should I be worried?"

He shrugged and looked away. "No reason." He adjusted his glasses again. "I mean, it's just that, you know, Jeff doesn't really like you all that much. He would probably recommend you go first. And it's not like…"

"Not like what?" I asked.

"Nothing." He glanced down. "Looks like it's break time." He disappeared behind the cubicle wall, leaving me to wonder what he was about to say. After a moment, I gave up because, after all, it was three o'clock, and three o'clock was break time. I locked my workstation and made my way back to the cafeteria, where I purchased a Twix bar from Marge.

I exited the building and made my way around to a bench that sat on a short gravel path just off the sidewalk in a small garden, facing a statue of the Virgin Mary. It was one of my favorite places to take a break and sometimes even eat lunch, when the weather wasn't oppressively hot or freezing cold. It wasn't for any religious reasons that I liked it. It was just peaceful. No one tended to bother you when you were sitting in front of a statue of the Virgin Mary. I wasn't sure why, but I didn't feel the need to question it.

As I approached, a young boy sat on one end of the bench. *Great.* I was about to turn around, but I didn't want to go back inside. I seriously needed to decompress for the measly fifteen minutes I was allowed, four of which were already gone. Besides, the kid's parents must be close by. They would probably be rounding him up any minute now. I mean, what kind of parent leaves a kid that looked to be about eight years old just sitting by himself outside a hospital?

"Mind if I have a seat?" I asked as I approached.

The kid didn't respond. He just slid over closer to the armrest, practically crawling up on it.

"Thanks," I said as I sat down.

I pulled the Twix from my pocket and tore it open, then slid one of the bars out of the wrapper and took a bite. Delicious. Twix was my one guilty pleasure.

Out of the corner of my eye, I saw the kid staring at the candy bar in my hand. I tried to ignore him and continue eating, but it didn't work.

"Nice weather we're having, huh?" I observed, hoping to take his stare away from my Twix. He shrugged and looked down at the ground. Mission accomplished. I took another bite. My God it was so tasty, but I was still distracted by the kid. So much for decompressing. By the time I finished the first bar, I noticed the kid staring again. I left the second bar inside the wrapper for the moment, feeling like I couldn't properly savor it until the kid was gone. Where were his parents, anyway? I glanced around but there was no one lingering nearby. Maybe they were in the lobby, picking up Grandma or someone and would be out shortly.

I took a deep breath and let it out slowly. The kid

kicked at the gravel some more, but still eyed my Twix.

I realized that my break was ruined and that a parent wasn't going to show up in time for me to salvage any of it, so I figured I might as well cut my losses.

I held out the remaining Twix. "You want what's left?"

The kid's eyes brightened noticeably, but he hesitated, not saying anything. I waved the bar a bit. "It's all yours if you want it."

He took it from me and practically inhaled it.

"Geez, don't choke on it," I warned.

The kid didn't reply. He just kept chewing until the bar was completely gone with one big swallow.

"Pretty good, huh?"

He nodded vigorously.

I checked my watch. I still had a few minutes, but of course there was no point in staying around. My Twix was gone.

"Well, nice talking to you, but I have to get back to work." I stood up. "By the way, taking candy from strangers is usually frowned upon by parents."

I thought I saw a small grin before I turned away.

Back inside, I managed to pass the time uninterrupted until five o'clock mercifully arrived. I locked my computer and grabbed my keys from my desk drawer. As I left, I saw Amy enter Jeff's office and close the door behind her. She was apparently having to stay late, and, to top it off, she was having to deal with Jeff, poor girl. That was a double whammy. It was very likely this would leave her in a bad mood for the evening that just might carry over to tomorrow. I made a mental note to tread carefully in the morning.

The short drive to my apartment was marginally enjoyable. It was mid-May and the weather had yet to turn uncomfortably hot, which was good because the air conditioner in my aging Ford Explorer was on the fritz. When I pulled into the parking lot, I looked for Sara's white Camry, but it was nowhere to be seen. She either had to stay late or she had errands to run before heading home. It was just as well. She would probably try to get me to go for a run with her, and I would have to come up with an excuse as to why there was no way in Hell I would do that. Also, it was Wednesday and that was Star Trek: Enterprise night. The show was in its second season and it was awesome. It was my one guilty pleasure.

After scraping together a sandwich and catching up on laundry, I wasted the rest of my evening on the web and watching TV until I fell asleep on the couch.

Chapter 2

Thursday, May 16th, 2002

The next morning, I woke up to the blaring of my alarm. I had moved from the couch to my bed somewhere in the middle of the night and had luckily managed to set the alarm in the process. After a quick shower and breakfast, I got dressed and once again waded into the sea of terrible drivers that stood between me and the hospital.

When I walked into the technology room, I risked a glance at Amy. She was busy typing away on her keyboard, and I wondered if I should venture a quick hello, but I recalled her walking into Jeff's office yesterday and assumed she would still be in a bad mood. I know I would have been, so I kept walking.

As soon as I sat down in my chair, Chip's giant face appeared over the cubicle wall.

"Did you see the email?"

"I just got here. I haven't even logged in yet," I said, trying not to sound annoyed. As brilliant as Chip was, he sometimes missed the most obvious things.

"Check your email," he insisted.

"Okay," I said, thinking he would sink out of sight and give me some time to do just that, but he stayed put. I sighed as I logged in and opened my email. I glanced through the usual automated reports and log alerts, along with an email announcing a meeting at 2 p.m. Nothing seemed out of the ordinary.

"What do you think?" he asked.

"About what?"

"The meeting."

I shrugged. I wasn't sure what he wanted from me. "What about it?"

He glanced back toward Jeff's office, then whispered, "I bet it's about the layoffs."

I nodded. "Ah, maybe so."

"Aren't you worried?" he asked. "We could be going home at the end of the day without a job."

I almost laughed out loud but caught myself. "Chip, nothing moves that fast around here."

"It does when it affects the bottom line," he said. "And from what I hear, the bottom line isn't too good lately."

"We're a nonprofit hospital," I reminded him. "How good could the bottom line ever be?"

The question was rhetorical, of course, but Chip seemed prepared to answer. Before he could get a word out, I held up a finger.

"I've got to stop you there, Chip. These logs aren't going to check themselves."

"I'm telling you," he insisted, once again glancing in the direction of Jeff's office, "it's going to happen."

"Okay, then," I said. "I've got work to do."

He sank out of sight, and I wished for the thousandth time in my career at St. Edwards that I had a different cube neighbor. Although maybe I was being hard on him. He was a good guy, unlike Jeff, who was a complete tool.

****

I spent the rest of the morning avoiding my coworkers as much as I possibly could by staying buried in performance monitors and logs. I also had several new user accounts to provision.

At 10 a.m., Jeff called a meeting of the infrastructure team to go over the details of a pending server migration project. The first phase of the plan called for the implementation of a new storage platform, which would happen over the upcoming weekend and, thankfully, did not involve me. The data would be kept in sync with the live copy in preparation for the server move, which would happen at the end of the following weekend, starting on Friday night and running into Saturday and, hopefully, be completed and tested by Saturday morning. It was going to suck. I was going to handle the setup and promotion of the new domain controllers and work with the programming team to move HERK, the aforementioned bane of my existence. Prior to then, I had to have the new servers installed, configured, and waiting for the starting pistol to sound.

When the meeting concluded, it was time for lunch, so I headed to the cafeteria. As usual, I ordered a grilled ham and cheese with fries and Dr. Pepper, then joined Sara, who sat at our usual table reading through a medical journal.

"Well, I have to work the weekend after next," I complained as I plopped down in the hard, plastic chair. "That's going to be so much fun."

"Mmmm hmmm," Sara said as she turned the page, not paying attention to me. How rude.

"I also won the lottery, so you're going to have to find a new lunch partner," I said.

"Mmmm hmmm."

I tapped on the table next to the journal. "Hello?"

She looked up. "What?"

"Are you even listening to me?"

"Of course," she lied.

"What did I say?"

She shrugged. "Something about the lottery next weekend?"

Close enough. "Whatcha readin'?"

She looked back down at the journal. "An article on that new cancer trial I was telling you about."

"Sounds exciting. Can I borrow it when you're done?"

She gave me a look that subtly said to stop being an idiot. I decided to press on with my complaining.

"So, Chip is freaking out this morning. The entire IT department is having a meeting at two, and he's worried he's going to be laid off by the end of the day."

Sara closed the journal and looked perplexed. "You know, we're having a meeting today at two as well."

"About what?" I asked.

"The memo didn't say, just that it was mandatory. I wonder if the other departments are also meeting. If they are, that's a bad sign."

I thought for a moment. Maybe it was a bad sign, but who knew. Besides, I felt totally secure. Well, mostly secure.

"So, what's the deal with the cancer trial?" I asked, against my better judgment.

Sara perked up again. "There is a study that is going to trial that looks very promising for women with triple negative invasive ductal carcinoma. It's simple, really. They are able to target tumors through drugs encapsulated inside liposomes. The breast is then heated up in what is basically a hot tub, which causes the drug to leak out of the liposomes. Isn't that amazing?"

"Yes." I nodded as though it all made sense to me.

"Researchers have been able to deliver thirty times the normal amount of drugs directly to the tumor without poisoning the rest of the body. It's very interesting." She paused to take a bite of celery smeared with peanut butter.

"We have this patient who recently relapsed for the second time. She's been through the wringer over the last six years. I'm hoping she can get in. It may not help her, but she's running out of time and options. It may just be her best shot at beating it."

"Wow. She's relapsed twice in six years? How old is she?"

"She's only thirty-one," Sara answered.

Geez. Only thirty-one and she's already spent six years of her life fighting breast cancer. Talk about getting the short end of the stick. The short, sharp, shit-covered end of the stick.

At that moment, Marge arrived with my food, setting the tray in front of me.

"Enjoy," she said, as she usually did. "See you at three."

"You know it," I replied out of habit.

We spent the remaining time making sporadic small talk as we ate, and Sara continued reading the medical journal. When time came to head back to work, I stood and grabbed my tray.

"Let me know how the meeting goes."

"Same here," she said, packing her various

containers back into her lunch sack.

I dumped my trash, stacked my tray with the others, and went back to my cubicle.

As I entered the IT room, I almost ran headlong into Amy.

"Watch where you're going, please," she instructed in a very non-polite manner, despite using the word please.

"Sorry," I mumbled as I looked at my feet. She was definitely in a bad mood from working late yesterday with Jeff. I moved out of her way and continued on to my desk.

It was just past one when Chip's giant head appeared above my monitor. "Less than an hour until the hammer drops."

"What does that mean?" I asked.

"You know, the meeting."

"I think you mean until the axe falls."

He thought a moment. "The axe falls? Are you sure?"

I shook my head. "No, I'm not. How about you go look it up?"

He sank out of view as I began to requisition the appropriate licensing for the new servers I needed to commission. At five 'til two, I stopped what I was doing as I noticed my coworkers beginning to make their way to the conference room across the hall. I stood and stretched, then bent over and locked my workstation. When I straightened up, Chip appeared.

"Looks like it's time," he said. He looked as though he was about to be sick. "By the way, you were right."

"About what?" I asked as we joined the exodus.

"It's generally referred to as the axe falling instead of the hammer, although it has a similar connotation, but overwhelmingly it's the axe that falls, not the hammer."

Dear God. "Did you spend this whole time researching that?" I asked.

"Of course not. I did some actual work as well."

There was standing room only when Chip and I entered the conference room, so we made our way to the back wall and found a space to stand. A few moments later, the murmur of conversation died down as the IT Director, a nice enough guy named Rick Mason, entered the room.

I had only talked with Mr. Mason on a few occasions. He spent most of his time doing higher level functions that required him to be anywhere but down in the trenches with the rest of us. He was the guy who Jeff reported to, and of course, I was the guy who reported to Jeff, as much as I disliked the arrangement.

Mr. Mason scrubbed a hand through his gray hair and pulled at the collar of his shirt. He adjusted his tie and cleared his throat.

"Hello, everyone. I'm going to cut straight to the chase here. I know there have been some rumors going around about possible layoffs. Well, it's true."

I heard a small groan escape from Chip. "I knew it," he whispered amid the sudden chatter in the room.

"Hang on," said Mr. Mason, holding his hands up to quiet the restless natives. "Just hear me out. We aren't being hit as hard as some of the other departments, but neither are we completely immune. We are being pushed to tighten our belts, so that's what we have to do. The good news is, the upcoming projects are all still on the table. The storage and server migrations are still on, as are the switch upgrades. Once those are finished, though, we will have to re-evaluate where we stand and determine what measures, if any, are needed to reduce the bottom line. I'll be working with the supervisors over the next week or so to figure out what we need to do and when. Once we know, we will let you know. Unfortunately, that's all the information I have for you at this moment. I don't want to keep you any longer. If you have any questions or concerns, come see me. Otherwise, try not to worry. We are going to do our best."

With that, he turned and walked out, gone almost as quickly as he had appeared.

"Wow," said Chip; the conversation in the room started back up. "I am so screwed."

"No you're not," I insisted. "You'll be fine."

Chip shook his head. "There are two of us in my position. I have the least seniority." He looked like he was about to faint as we joined the line of people leaving the room. I stayed to Chip's left and slightly behind him in case he did indeed faint. It was the perfect getaway position. I didn't want him landing on me.

"Even so," I continued, "they can't allow someone as smart as you to get away. And I'm sure security will be a priority. There's no way they could afford a breach, so there's no way they are going to get rid of you."

As we crossed the hall back into the IT room, Chip shrugged. "I don't know. Maybe you're right. I sure hope you are, anyway."

"Of course, I'm right," I assured him. "If they are

going to layoff anyone, it would be me. I mean, I can basically be replaced with a handful of scripts."

It was that moment I realized I could be replaced with a handful of scripts. Shit. In the process of trying to keep Chip from blacking out and hitting the floor, I inadvertently triggered some worries of my own.

In my cube, I sat down and stared at my monitor, trying to convince myself that I couldn't be replaced that easily. I was exceedingly thankful when the time hit three o'clock.

I stood up from my desk, walked past Amy without staring too much in her direction, and headed to the cafeteria, where I purchased my Twix bar, then proceeded to my outdoor sanctuary.

As I approached the Virgin Mary, I was frustrated to see the kid was back on my bench, head down, kicking at the gravel.

I paused and thought about turning around and going back to the cafeteria, but I immediately nixed that idea. The bench was my sanctuary, my place to decompress, if only for a bit, so that I could make it to quitting time. And it was my special place where I could enjoy my one guilty pleasure: a Twix bar. There was no way I was going to let some brat take that away from me. I walked over to the bench and stopped.

"Back again, huh?" I asked.

He nodded without looking up at me but, instead, fixated on the candy bar in my hand.

"Mind if I join you?"

No answer, he just once again slid farther against the arm of the bench so he was practically sitting on it.

I sat down, still holding the Twix in my hand, his eyes locked on it. Just great. I tore open the package and pulled out one of the bars, then held out the package.

"You want the rest?" I asked. The words had no sooner left my mouth when he grabbed the package and extricated the remaining bar.

"Go easy," I said. "Try to at least taste it on the way down."

He slowed a bit, but still lit into the bar with an impressive amount of gusto. I shook my head, sighed, and tried to enjoy the half of the bar I was left with. Half a Twix. It was no way to live.

When I was finished, well after the kid had finished his half, I sat in silence, staring at the statue and wondering if someone was going to show up to take the kid away; they never did.

As my break neared its end, I stood up just as the kid wadded up the package and dropped it on the ground.

"What are you doing?" I asked. He shrugged. "Other people use this Earth. You can't be trashing it up for the rest of us. It's not cool."

He leaned down and grabbed the wrapper, looked at it in his hand, and appeared to be thinking. After a moment, he started to stuff it in his pocket. I sighed again and held out my hand.

"Here." I closed and reopened my outstretched palm. He hesitated a moment before slowly handing me the wrapper. On my way back into the building, I dropped it into a trash can next to the door. "Kids these days," I muttered to myself.

****

Back at my desk, I traded emails with Steve, who was handling the data sync. He sent me the paths I

21

would need for the new servers, which I dumped into a highly unorganized folder on my desktop labeled "New Server Stuff." At a quarter to five, against my better judgement, I started burning the disc I would need to install the operating system on the new servers. I hoped it would be done by five, but my hopes were dashed when five o'clock came around and the disc was only eighty percent complete. I didn't want to lock my workstation and leave it running, risking having to go through the process again in the morning, so I watched as the percentage slowly counted up and the room began emptying out.

When the disc finished burning and verifying, it was almost fifteen after. I leaned over and glanced around the wall of my cubicle. The only person in sight was Amy. Maybe my luck was about to change. I quickly removed the disc from the drive, slipped it into a paper sleeve, and dropped it into my desk drawer. As I was about to stand, I heard Jeff's voice. I leaned out and saw him talking to Amy. Neither seemed to be aware that I was still there, so I ducked back just enough to still see what was going on, but hopefully not be noticed. I could just make out what he was saying.

"I'm afraid I need to see you in my office," he told her. The poor girl. That would make two evenings in a row.

"Oh, am I in trouble?" she asked, but it sounded flirty. It was probably the acoustics in the room playing tricks on me.

"We'll see," Jeff said. They both laughed as they started toward his office. I watched them disappear inside and close the door.

I stood, hoping Amy wasn't in too much trouble,

and quietly made my way out of the IT room, making a mental note to once again tread carefully in the morning. Amy would surely be in a bad mood after having to stay late two evenings in a row. I wasn't feeling too great myself, having gone fifteen minutes over.

****

When I reached the parking lot, I saw Sara about to climb into her car. I waved and yelled to get her attention. She looked around, saw me, and waited.

"How did the meeting go?" I asked as I approached.

"Looks like the rumors were true. They're expecting some cutbacks."

"Same for us," I said as I leaned against her car and crossed my arms. "Chip is really freaking out now."

"Why do you keep telling me about Chip? I don't even know him."

"You're not missing anything," I assured her. "So, do you think you'll be safe?"

She shrugged. "I don't know. I have the most seniority of the research assistants, but who knows if they won't lay all of us off?"

I waved a dismissive hand. "I'm sure you'll be fine. There's no way they would get rid of you."

She smiled. "I wish I could be so sure."

"Well, if you get the boot, you can always live in your car until you find something else."

"I still have a lot of payments left on this thing. If I get the boot, I won't have a car for very long."

"I see. In that case, you can sleep in my car," I offered. "Just be out each morning by the time I go to work."

"You are too kind. Now, stop leaning on my car. I don't want you to scratch the paint with your abrasive personality."

I laughed as I stepped away. "Your sharp wit is probably more of a danger than my personality."

"Funny," she said without laughing.

I looked across the lot at my dusty Explorer. "I don't suppose you want to give me a lift to my car?"

"Now *that's* funny." This time, she was actually laughing.

"No? Okay then. See you tomorrow at lunch?"

"Sure," she said as she opened the door to her car. "Hey, you want to grab a bite to eat this evening?"

"No thanks," I answered. "I'll probably hit a drive-thru on the way, or just fix a sandwich when I get home."

"Okay. See you tomorrow." She got in and shut the door. As she pulled away, I couldn't believe she wasn't going to give me a ride to my car. How rude. I sighed and started walking. It really wasn't too far, but it was the principle of the matter.

When I reached the Explorer, I noticed a new ding on the driver side door. *Just great. There goes the resale value.*

I climbed in, cranked the engine to life, and pulled through the empty spot in front of me. As I was navigating my way toward the exit, I noticed Jeff and Amy leaving the building. They were both smiling and talking. Maybe whatever it was that Jeff had needed to talk to her about had turned out to be nothing big. Or maybe she was just kissing up to Jeff, who, by the way, was a complete tool. I shook my head and continued on.

Chapter 3

Friday, May 17th, 2002

When my alarm sounded, I had to fight the urge to throw it against the wall. Lucky for it, it was Friday and that, at least, was somewhat of a consolation.

I showered and ate breakfast, noting that I needed to restock the refrigerator at some point before the weekend was over.

The drive across town was surprisingly enjoyable, and I was actually starting to feel pretty good about the day. I even smiled at a few people as I made my way into the building. When I reached the IT room, I paused for a moment and tried to think of something charming and funny to say to Amy. Unfortunately, I was drawing a complete blank. I took a deep breath and entered, but Amy wasn't at her desk. It was just as well, I guess. As I walked to my cubicle, I saw her alone in the kitchen, fixing a cup of coffee. It seemed like the perfect opportunity to make a little small talk, maybe throw in a hint or two about having nothing to do over the weekend and see what might happen.

She glanced at me as I entered.

"Morning," I said.

"Morning," she echoed. So far, so good.

She tore open a packet of sugar and dumped it into her cup. Even though I hated coffee, I grabbed a

Styrofoam cup from the stack next to the coffeemaker and managed to fill it without spilling anything. I watched as Amy started adding creamer to hers.

"Wow," I observed. "Sugar *and* creamer."

She paused and looked at me, blank-faced.

"That's a lot of, uh…" I froze, unable to think of anything witty. "…added…flavor."

She sighed, which reminded me of Sara's annoying habit. It must be a woman thing.

"So, what do you think about the possible layoffs?" I asked, neatly rescuing the moment.

"I have work to do," she replied, taking her coffee and leaving.

"Yep," I said quietly to no one. "Me, too." I dumped my coffee in the sink and went to my desk, grabbed the disc I had created the day before, and made my way down to the data center in the basement. After locating the rack with the new servers, I slid out the KVM drawer and popped open the screen. I selected the first server and loaded the disc into its CD drive, hit the power button, and spent the rest of the morning installing and getting the servers connected so I could resume configuring them from my desk.

****

When lunch time arrived, I went to the cafeteria, where I acquired the necessary sustenance I needed to survive. I already had my food and was taking the first bite as Sara arrived.

She plopped down in the seat across the table and began opening her lunch bag somewhat aggressively.

"What's up with you?" I asked.

"Dr. Carver. I don't think he's going to recommend Amelia for the clinical trial that just might be her only hope."

"I see," I said, nodding. "And who is Amelia?"

"She's the patient I was telling you about yesterday."

"Ah yes. The one that's in for the third time in, what, six years?"

Sara nodded as she ripped open a container of some sort of gross health food that she had fished out of her lunch bag. I watched in horror as she began eating. I really needed to get a new lunch partner.

"Why won't he recommend her?" I asked.

"Because he thinks it might be too late, that someone else would be a better test case."

"I see, I see." I asked the next question very carefully. "And is it too late?"

She looked up from her food, but the anger drained from her face. She looked tired and sad. And, I was surprised to notice, beautiful.

"Probably," she confessed. "But I'm trying to persuade him to recommend her based on the fact that a proper clinical trial should include late stage patients as well. Who's to say a treatment that doesn't work well for early stage patients won't make a difference for late stagers? What if a treatment that would have reversed late-stage cancer gets discarded because the trial was biased to the earlier stages? We should cover all the bases. I mean, sure, it's up to those that are running the trial, but at the very least, he could make an argument for her."

She slumped in her seat and stared at her food. I wished there were something that I could do to help, but I knew there wasn't, so I ate some more of my sandwich.

After several minutes of silence, Sara finally spoke.

"I'm heading home this weekend. You want to come along? My parents were asking about you the other day."

By home, I knew Sara meant Webbers Falls, where she had grown up and where her parents still lived. The small town was located across the border in Oklahoma, about an hour away from Fort Smith. And when I say small, I mean small.

Since moving back to Fort Smith, I would periodically ride along with Sara on her visits home. She went most weekends, and I tagged along every now and then. It had been a while since I had gone, so it seemed like a good idea. After all, I would be working the following weekend, so a small getaway would probably do me some good.

"Sure, I'll go," I agreed. "You staying over?"

She nodded.

"I'll bring a bag, then."

****

After lunch, I focused on configuring the new servers from my desk, only having to make one trip down to the basement to fix an issue. Chip had appeared briefly to ask me how it was going but, otherwise, I was mercifully left alone.

When three o'clock arrived, I locked my workstation, picked up a Twix from Marge, and headed out to the bench.

As I approached, I stopped in frustration when I saw the kid sitting there, kicking at the gravel. This was getting out of hand.

"Christ," I muttered under my breath as I turned around and went back inside. I purchased a second

Twix from Marge and went back out.

"We gotta stop meeting like this," I said as I neared the bench. The kid slid over without prompting. I pulled the second Twix out of my pocket and held it out. He took it without a word and began tearing at the package.

"Okay, we have to set some ground rules here. If you are going to eat a Twix in my presence, you need to do it the right way." I tore open my Twix and slid one bar halfway out. The kid followed my lead.

"You can't just inhale the thing," I continued. "You have to savor it. Give it the proper respect it deserves. What you do is take a bite, but don't start chewing it up right away. You have to let the chocolate melt just a bit in your mouth, then slowly chew it. Savor every moment."

I took a bite and the kid followed suit. I waited, wondering if he could actually hold out and not start immediately chomping away. To my surprise, he didn't chew until I started.

We sat in silence, properly eating our candy bars and staring at the Virgin Mary. Once the bars were gone and my break was approaching its time limit, I stood up and held out my hand. He placed his wrapper in it.

"See ya, kid," I said and turned to go. As I walked away, I heard him speak for the first time.

"Bye."

****

Back at my desk, I alternated between applying updates to one of the new servers and watching the clock. Neither of them was noticeably moving. Just as I had come to the conclusion that both were stopped cold, Chip appeared above my monitor.

"You got any plans this evening?" he asked.

I kept staring at my monitor. "I'm busy."

In my peripheral vision, I could see a confused look cross his face.

"Are you?" he asked.

"Of course, I am," I countered, looking up at him. "Why wouldn't I be?"

"It's just that you looked like you were about to fall asleep."

"Things aren't always what they appear," I told him, not fully expecting him to grasp that concept. "But if you must know, I don't have plans."

As soon as the words left my mouth, I had a sudden feeling of foreboding. I hoped he wasn't about to invite himself over to my apartment where he would, no doubt, bore me to death by endlessly complaining about work and the possible layoffs.

"I'm thinking I might hit some of the job boards, just see what's out there," he said, and I breathed a sigh of relief.

"Good luck." I focused on my monitor and hoped he would get the hint.

"How are the servers coming along?" he asked, totally not getting the hint.

"So far, so good," I said. "But if you don't mind, I really need to focus here."

Just as Chip was about to speak again, something caught his attention over his shoulder.

I leaned out around my cubicle wall and saw Amy walking toward us.

"Hi, Amy," Chip and I greeted her in unison as she neared. I gave him a quick glare, but he was too busy practically drooling over her to notice.

"Hey, Chip," she said with a smile as she passed by. I could only assume she hadn't heard me. She seemed to be in a better mood than previous days, but it was Friday after all, and surely Jeff wasn't going to keep her after work for a third straight day, which had to be a big relief for her.

Chip opened his mouth to speak again, but I quickly interrupted.

"I gotta get back to work here, if you don't mind."

Chip nodded. "No problem. I need to wrap up a few things myself." He sank out of sight.

What felt like hours later, the clock finally clicked over to 4:45. It wasn't quite quitting time, but it was close enough. I stood and stretched, taking the opportunity to look around the room. Everyone seemed to be busy, which was unusual for a Friday. They were likely just trying to kiss up to Jeff, hoping he would put in a good word for them if the layoffs happened. I contemplated doing the same, or at least pretending to do the same, when I saw Amy at her desk and changed my mind. Since she was in a great mood, this would be the perfect opportunity to chat her up a bit, maybe drop a hint about not having any plans for the weekend. I remembered I had told Sara I would go with her to Webbers Falls, but I'm sure she would understand if by some miracle I wound up with a date with Amy.

I locked my workstation and nonchalantly exited my cubicle.

"See you next week," Chip practically yelled as I walked by. I flinched and looked around to see how much attention he had drawn, but luckily everyone was still busy trying to impress the boss.

I gave Chip a quick wave and a stern look before

continuing on.

As I neared Amy's desk, I took a deep breath to calm my nerves.

"Hi, Amy."

She glanced up from her monitor.

"Any big plans for the weekend?" I asked.

I detected a small shake of her head as she resumed typing.

"Yeah, me neither," I said. "I'm just going to hang out, not do much."

She stopped working and stood up. "Have fun with that." She brushed past me and headed for the kitchen.

I nodded and watched her walk away. I contemplated following her to extend our conversation because it seemed to be heading in a good direction, but I didn't want to push my luck, so I ducked out the door and headed for the parking lot.

When I reached my Explorer, I saw Sara's car still parked three spots down from mine. She was probably working right up until five. I thought about waiting around to plan out our departure time in the morning, but that would have defeated the purpose of leaving early. I once again noticed the new ding on the door as I climbed in, started the engine, and drove away.

***

Sometime later, I was awakened by the ringing of my cell phone. As I opened my eyes, my apartment was already dark, lit only by the glow of the TV. I picked up the phone to see Sara's name on the screen.

I hit the answer button. "What's up?"

"Hey," she replied. "You sound like you were asleep."

"I was," I said as I sat up, grabbed the remote from

the overpriced coffee table, and muted the TV.

"It's only 8:30," she pointed out.

I held my phone out and looked at the time on the screen before returning it to my ear.

"So it is. Is there something I can help you with?"

"I was just calling to see if you were still going home with me."

"Yep."

"Good. I was thinking we could head out about 10 o'clock in the morning. Or we could get an earlier start and go grab some breakfast at Calico County, if you can manage to drag yourself out of bed."

The occasional breakfast at Calico County was my one guilty pleasure. Just the thought of it made my mouth water.

"This earlier start thing doesn't sound good at all," I said, "but, as you know, I can never resist breakfast at Calico."

"That's why I offered." I could practically hear the smug grin in her voice.

"Fine," I agreed. "I'm in."

"Good, I'll see you in the parking lot at, say, 9 a.m. sharp."

"You know, I'm not comfortable with you exploiting my weaknesses in order to get me out of bed early on a weekend."

She laughed, apparently thinking I was joking, even though I was entirely serious.

"If you aren't at my car at 9 o'clock, you're buying," she warned.

"Challenge accepted. See you at 8:59."

After hanging up, I laid back down on the couch and stared at the TV, replaying my late-day conversation with Amy over in my head. *Have fun*, she had said. If that wasn't flirting, I didn't know what was.

Chapter 4

Saturday, May 18th, 2002

That morning, I went through my usual routine of cursing the alarm clock and hitting the snooze button a few times until begrudgingly crawling out of bed. I had purposely set the alarm much earlier than needed, just to prove a point to Sara that I could be on time. After showering and getting dressed, I quickly packed an overnight bag and rushed out the door at exactly 8:49.

Sara's apartment was on the far side of the next building over from mine. I was leaning casually against the hood of her car when she rounded the corner nine minutes later, carrying her usual pink duffel bag.

"What did I tell you about the paint?" she called out as she approached.

"Oh, I'm sorry," I said. "It's just that I've been out here so long my legs were getting tired, so I had to prop myself up."

She arched an eyebrow and gave me a skeptical look. "If your legs can't hold you up for more than a minute and a half, you need to start exercising."

I stood up straight as she unlocked the doors with the remote.

"A minute and a half? I'm offended by that," I said as I walked around to the passenger side. "I lasted at least two minutes."

She grinned as we opened the doors and put our bags in the back seat.

We had an unspoken agreement that we would always take her car when traveling together, mostly because we wanted to be able to make it back and that could sometimes be iffy with my Explorer. This was especially true on longer drives, but it held even if we were only going a few blocks. There was also the fact that she was not a fan of my driving ability. I had given up trying to convince her otherwise long ago, when her argument that I was prone to road rage was validated on a few occasions.

"I hope you brought your purse," I said as we climbed in and closed the doors. "I'm famished this morning."

"What makes you think I'm paying?" she asked.

"We had a bet," I reminded her.

We latched our seatbelts and she started the car. "There was no bet," she argued. "We just agreed that you would pay if you were late."

"I don't recall agreeing to anything."

She looked over at me. "Ah, so you admit we never agreed to anything, which would include a bet."

I hated it when she did that. "Just drive," I said. "And try not to kill us."

The short drive from our apartments to Calico County was uneventful, with the exception of Sara slapping my hand away from the radio when I reached for it. For all her good qualities, her taste in music was not one of them.

When we reached the restaurant, its small parking lot was full, so we parked in front of a pet store just next door in a tiny strip mall. Despite the crowds, there was no wait. The hostess, a young, attractive girl with long, shiny brown hair, led us to a booth.

"Your server will be right with you," she said with a practiced smile and walked away. I watched her go without being too obvious about it, but when I looked across the table at Sara, she was staring at me with her eyebrows raised.

"What?" I asked.

"You see something you like?"

I picked up my menu, despite the fact I already knew what I was going to order, and began flipping through it.

"I don't know what you're talking about," I said.

So much for not being obvious. Luckily, our waitress arrived to take our drink order. She, too, was young and attractive, but through great effort, I managed not to glance her way more than once as she left.

"Wow," said Sara.

"Oh, come on. I barely even noticed."

"Noticed what?"

I started to answer, but realized it was probably some sort of trick question, so I went back to studying the menu until the waitress returned with our glasses of orange juice. She took our orders. I chose my usual of two scrambled eggs, three pieces of bacon, and a biscuit with gravy, known as *The Traditional*. Sara, of course, chose an egg-white omelet from the *Healthy Selections* section. At least it wasn't broccoli or some type of weed. I handed my menu over as I stared directly into Sara's eyes and stayed locked in, even as the waitress walked away.

Sara grinned. "That must have been tough."

"You have no idea. Oh hey, speaking of, I had a great conversation with Amy yesterday."

Sara rolled her eyes. "Here we go again," she groaned.

"No, seriously," I continued unabated, "she wished me a good weekend."

"Oh really?" Sara raised an eyebrow. She seemed somehow unconvinced.

"Yes, really. Well, basically. She told me to have fun."

"Have fun?"

I nodded.

"And what were you two talking about when she told you this?"

"We were talking about the weekend. I asked her if she had any plans. She said no, then I mentioned I didn't have any plans either."

"Wait," Sara interrupted, gesturing first to the room around us then to herself. "You did have plans. You know, with me."

I waved a dismissive hand. "Right, but she didn't know that."

"So?" countered Sara. She seemed to be getting a little irritated for some reason. Perhaps I wasn't properly explaining things.

"Because she wasn't doing anything, I told her I wasn't doing anything either. You see, I was planting the seed that maybe we could do something together. And besides, if she had wanted to get together, I knew you would understand."

Sara sighed and shook her head. "So, where does the *have fun* part come in?"

"After I told her I wasn't doing anything, that's

when she told me to have fun."

She still looked confused about the whole situation. "What were her exact words?"

I shrugged. "It was something like, 'Have fun with that.'"

"Have fun with that?"

I nodded.

"Then what?"

"Then she got up from her desk and walked away."

Sara lowered her head into her hands and stayed that way for a moment before looking up at me.

"Okay, let me get this straight. She told you she wasn't doing anything this weekend. Then you told her you weren't doing anything this weekend. Then she said, 'Have fun with that' and walked away."

I nodded. "That's pretty much it, yes."

She sighed and shook her head. "Unbelievable," she muttered.

"I know," I said. "Pretty cool, huh? I really think she likes me."

****

When our food arrived, I ate with the proper amount of gusto reserved for an amazing breakfast. Around bites, I filled Sara in on just how terrible Jeff was and how much it was going to suck having to work the following weekend. When we were finished eating, I grabbed the ticket from the table, and we walked to the front. Sara pulled some cash out of her front pocket and started to hand it to me to cover her part of the check, but I waved it off.

"I got it," I insisted.

"You weren't late. You don't have to pay for mine."

"I know," I said. I paid for both meals and left a generous tip.

"Thanks," Sara offered as we exited the restaurant. "That was *actually* nice of you."

"That would have sounded better if you hadn't emphasized the word actually."

We both laughed. "Fair enough. I suppose the large tip had nothing to do with how attractive our waitress was?"

"Of course not," I said, offended. "It was based solely on the high level of service."

"She never refilled your orange juice," Sara pointed out.

I shrugged. "I wasn't that thirsty anyway."

We climbed into the car, buckled in, and I reached for the radio, only to have my hand slapped away again. I settled into my seat, resigning myself to top forty hits for the next hour or so. A few months earlier, I had passed on purchasing Apple's newest product, a personal music player called the iPod, because of its four-hundred-dollar price tag. I was beginning to regret that decision.

As we pulled onto Rogers Avenue and headed west, I leaned my seat back and watched the world pass by outside my window. A few minutes later when we made a slight right onto Garrison Avenue and into the heart of the old downtown, I was already feeling sleepy. The warm sun combined with the large breakfast was taking its toll on my consciousness.

A short distance later, Fort Smith abruptly ended near the bank of the Arkansas River. As we crossed over the muddy waters, we left Arkansas behind and entered Oklahoma, passing through a short stretch of farmland before reaching the small town of Roland. It was there that we joined Interstate 40 and continued westward, staying more or less parallel to the river until we would cross it once more when we reached Webbers Falls.

Six miles from Roland, we passed by Muldrow. It was in that area that I dozed off and slept for the next forty minutes or so as we passed Sallisaw, which was followed by an uneventful stretch of road until Webbers Falls.

****

I awoke just as the bridge came into sight, arching up and over the Arkansas River. As we crossed, I looked out at the brown waters flowing lazily by, sixty feet below, and stretched my arms and legs as best as I could in the confined space.

"Did you have a nice nap?" Sara asked.

I turned my attention away from the waters and said, "As a matter of fact, I did. Did you have a nice drive?"

She nodded as she watched the road ahead. "It was nice and quiet."

I assumed that was meant as some sort of slight toward me, but I let it slide.

Two miles farther on, Sara took exit 287 and turned north onto Highway 100. Only a mile and a half up, Highway 100 joined with Old Highway 64 and cut back east toward the river, but rather than continue, we turned right onto the small road that quickly split into Weatherly Drive and Commercial Street, on which Sara's parents lived.

The town itself was small, with a population of fewer than seven hundred, and was the epitome of rural.

Other than another tiny town, Gore, which lay just across the river on Highway 64, there was nothing but flat farmland as far as the eye could see.

I stared blankly out the side window as we drove past the school and thought about reaching for the radio again, just to see if Sara was paying attention. We were only a few blocks from our destination. So even if she wasn't, I would have no time to find a decent station, if one even existed there. So I nixed the idea.

Moments later, Sara turned into the driveway of her parent's modest white house. A chain link fence ran around the small, well-kept lawn that her dad took great pride in. Their dog, a mutt named Max, bolted from the porch as soon as we exited the car.

"Hey, Maxey boy," I called to him as he jumped up on the fence, trying to reach us. His tail was wagging so fast I thought it might fly completely off.

As we were grabbing our bags from the backseat, I heard the screen door open. When I shut the car door and turned, Sara's dad was on the front porch.

"Max, get over here," he ordered, calling the dog to him so that we could get through the small gate without being harassed. The dog dutifully trotted over and sat down on the porch step.

"Hey, Mr. Bartlett," I said as I slung my bag over my shoulder and opened the gate for Sara.

"Eric, how are you? Haven't seen you in a while." Before I could answer he turned his attention to Sara. "And how's my girl?"

"Hi, Dad," she said, stepping up onto the porch. He embraced her in a giant bear hug, kissed her forehead, and turned and yelled through the door. "Dottie! The kids are home." Sara's mom immediately appeared from inside, pushing open the screen door.

"I'm right here, you don't have to yell," she said, smiling, as she swatted at his arm.

"Hey, Mom." Sara stepped around her father and gave her mother a hug.

If there was one thing I had learned about the Bartletts, it was that they liked to hug. They were also the kindest and warmest people I had ever met in my life.

Since hugging was never really my thing, Mr. Bartlett held out his hand, and I cringed inside. Charlie Bartlett was in his early 60s with gray hair, but he was by no means an old man. A lifetime of manual labor had left him with a bad shoulder and back, but it had also resulted in a powerful, stocky frame and a grip that could crush concrete blocks. I braced myself and grabbed his hand. Even though I knew what to expect, I was still always surprised by his strength.

"How's life treating you, Eric?" he asked as I tried not to scream out in pain.

"Fair enough, I suppose. Yourself?"

He let go of my hand, and I resisted the urge to cradle it against my body. "Can't complain."

Even though Mr. Bartlett innately understood my aversion to hugging, Sara's mom was an entirely different story. Even if she somehow knew, it never deterred her.

"Eric, what a nice surprise. It's good to see you. Where have you been hiding yourself?" she asked as she hugged me and kissed my cheek.

"Hey, Mrs. B. It's good to see you, too."

"We were beginning to think we would never see you again," she continued.

"No such luck," Sara said, grinning.

"Y'all come on in and make yourselves at home," insisted Mrs. Bartlett.

As everyone filed in, I stopped to pet Max, who was bouncing around at my feet.

"Hey, Max," I said as I knelt down. "Who's a good boy?" I scratched his ears as he attempted to lick my face, his tail still wagging uncontrollably. I stood up and followed everyone in, letting Max through the door with me.

As small as the Bartlett house was, it was a miracle that there were three bedrooms. The result was that every room in the house was undersized and there was only one bathroom. Having lived in an apartment for so long, I felt perfectly at home.

I followed Sara through the living room, expertly navigating the tight quarters, and into the hallway that led to the bedrooms and the bathroom. Sara's old room, the one she had grown up in, was the last on the left, and the guest room was directly across from it. We tossed our bags onto our respective beds and went back to the living room, where we sat on opposite ends of a dark green couch while Sara's parents sat down in their matching recliners. Max jumped up into Sara's lap and set about the task of trying to lick her face.

"Max, be good," she instructed, but not sternly. She was laughing as she dodged his attempts.

"That dog is pretty well worthless," said Mr. Bartlett.

Sara clamped her hands over Max's ears. "Don't you listen to him, Max. You're the best dog in the whole world." This only served to excite Max even more.

"Eric, what have you been up to since we last saw you?" Mr. Bartlett asked as Sara continued laughing and dodging Max's advances.

"The usual. Work. Speaking of which, I hear you're retired now."

He nodded. "Yep. Had to finally give in and retire early."

He didn't say why, but I assumed it had to do with his bad back. Or, maybe times were tough at Consolidated Grain and Barge, and he was forced into it. Either way, I was just making guesses.

Sara's mom chimed in. "Everyone at school has been giving me a hard time about being married to an old retiree," she told us with a smile. "I keep telling them I only look young, but I'm actually an old lady."

With her dark, shoulder length hair and smooth skin that only showed a few laugh lines, Mrs. Bartlett could easily pass for a woman in her early forties rather than mid-fifties. The age difference between the two of them did indeed look much greater than the eight years it actually was.

Max gave up trying to make out with Sara and settled in between us, laying his head on my leg.

"I bet Max here is grateful to have company all day now," I said, scratching his ears.

"Oh yes," Mr. Bartlett said. "He's just tickled pink. We even go out for walks on a regular basis now. We go down to the river, and I let him chase the geese a while, then we come back and take a nap."

The river was only about five blocks away but, being such a small town, practically everything was only five blocks away.

"How are things going at the hospital?" Mrs.

Bartlett asked. I wasn't sure if she was talking to me or Sara, but Sara beat me to the punch.

"It's going well," she said. She followed by raving about the new possible treatment for breast cancer and the early results. I assumed I was going to have to hear the entire story for the second time, but she stopped short of mentioning the young cancer patient who Dr. Carver had declined to recommend for the trial in Tulsa. I found that odd, since she had been pretty irritated about it the previous day.

We continued catching up and making small talk for a while until Sara stood up and announced she was going for a run. She went to her room to change as Mr. Bartlett stood up and said, "I think I'll go out and sit on the porch a spell." He looked in my direction. "Care to join me?"

"Sure," I said and followed him out the front door with Max in tow. Mr. Bartlett sat down in one of the two metal rocking chairs and I took the other. There was a small table in between us that held a potted plant.

"Nice day today," he pointed out.

I nodded. "Yup."

"How was the drive in?"

I shrugged. "Not sure. I slept for a good portion of it."

He chuckled and looked off to his left, in the direction of the silos that towered over the Consolidated Grain and Barge Company property.

"How's Sara getting along these days?" he asked, redirecting his gaze to Max, who laid down at his feet.

"Fine, I guess."

"I worry about her," he explained. "Living alone in the city."

I almost laughed at his characterization of Fort Smith as "the city", but I caught myself. To me, that term was reserved for actual cities with populations greater than Fort Smith's eighty thousand. Granted, it was no small town, but I just didn't see it as "the city".

"No need to worry," I assured him. "Sara is tough and smart. She can more than take care of herself."

"Still, I'm glad she's got you nearby."

At that, I did laugh out loud.

The screen door opened and Sara stepped out onto the porch, decked out in her running gear, which included undoubtedly expensive running shoes and knee-high compression socks, along with shorts and a tank top that were both, I suddenly realized while sitting next to her very strong father, way too small and tight. I made it a point not to look below her neck, just in case he was watching me. Not that I thought of Sara in that way, but it was better safe than sorry.

"What's so funny out here?" she asked.

"Oh, nothing much," her dad answered. I got the feeling that he didn't want her to know about our conversation.

"I was just telling your dad the one joke that I know," I lied to help cover our tracks.

Sara rolled her eyes. "Not the one about the jumper cables."

"The one and only."

She shook her head and turned to leave, bouncing down the two porch steps. "I'm assuming neither of you want to join me," she called over her shoulder as she opened the gate and stepped through, closing it behind her.

"You assume correctly," I said.

"In that case, I'll be back in a bit." She turned and jogged up the driveway, turning left and heading toward the river.

"Thanks for covering," Mr. Bartlett offered as I purposely looked away from where Sara was running. "I don't want her to worry about me worrying about her."

"No problem."

He paused a moment. "So, you've known each other a good long while now, right?"

I thought about it and quickly did the math in my head. "Somewhere around ten years."

"Ten years," he repeated and whistled. "That's quite a while."

I nodded.

"You know," he continued, "me and Dottie thought maybe you two were dating back in college but were just hiding it from us."

"What made you think that?" I asked, surprised.

"Oh, I don't know. I guess it was how she always talked about you with her mom. Even after you two graduated, she would still mention you every now and then. And when you moved back to Fort Smith and started coming here with her, we just assumed once again you two were an item."

That was all news to me.

"So, tell me," he said, turning toward me. "What exactly is the nature of your relationship with my daughter?"

To say I suddenly felt uncomfortable was an understatement. I cleared my throat while also preparing to make a run for it if he made any sudden moves. Even though he was the nicest man I knew and wouldn't harm a fly, I still thought, once again, that it was better safe than sorry.

"Believe me," I stammered, a bit nervously. "Sara and I are just friends. I've never thought of her in, you know, *that* way. I swear. We're just friends. In fact, she's my best friend in the world."

I was surprised by that last sentence, even as the words were leaving my mouth. It wasn't like I didn't have any other friends. I mean, there was Chip, I guess, and…other people who had come and gone over the years. But, since college, Sara had always just been there.

"Relax," Mr. Bartlett chuckled, obviously noticing my uneasiness. "I don't mean to give you the third degree here. Truth is, I would be tickled pink if you two kids got together. You're a good guy, Eric, and I happen to think you two would be perfect for each other."

"Well, sorry to disappoint you Mr. B., but we're just friends."

He nodded. "Fair enough."

We sat in silence for a while until Sara reappeared in the distance, jogging up the road toward us. I watched as she approached and had a sudden realization.

You know, he's right. I am a good guy.

****

That evening, we all piled into Sara's car, drove the five blocks across town to the Burger Barn, and had dinner. The Burger Barn had been around since the 1980s and, aside from a few fast food joints by the interstate, it was the only restaurant in town. Luckily, the food far exceeded my low standards and was, in fact, one of the things I looked forward to when coming to Webbers Falls.

After eating, we drove back to the Bartletts' house, where the four of us walked the few blocks down Commercial to the Showtime Event Center. Known as Showtime at The Falls, the event center was located in one of the handful of remaining old buildings that once comprised the main downtown area. The center, next door to what was an old pharmacy which housed the Webbers Falls Historic Museum, was a main attraction in the town. It was a surprisingly cool space, rustic and quaint, complete with a stage and tasteful lighting. The atmosphere was cozy and relaxing. Every other Saturday night, a local band would play as townsfolk danced and had a good time. And, surprisingly, the band was really good. The only problem was that they played country and western music, which was way down on my list of likes.

We arrived just after 8 p.m., Mr. Bartlett paid the cover charge for each of us, and we went inside and found an empty table. Sara and I were by far the youngest people in the room, as only the older residents of Webbers Falls seemed to be interested in attending the show. When the band started playing, Mr. and Mrs. Bartlett got up, along with most of the crowd of forty or fifty people, to dance. I took the opportunity to slip outside for a breath of fresh air, nodding greetings along the way to familiar faces whose names I could not remember. As I stepped outside, I glanced back to see Sara following behind me. We could still hear the muted sound of the band inside as the door closed.

"You didn't want to stay and dance?" Sara asked. It was a running joke. The last thing in the world I ever wanted to do was dance.

"Can't," I said. "Old polka injury."

The evening was warm, and the last few traces of light were fading away to the west. To our east, the river flowed by, less than a hundred yards away in the growing darkness.

"You wanna walk down to the dock?" I asked, wanting to get away from the music for a while.

"Lead the way," Sara said.

We walked east to the end of the block, where Commercial Street ended at River Road. Across River Road, Park Road dropped down a small slope into a parking area for the boat ramp and dock. The road itself turned left and headed north along the river into the City Park, where it looped around and came back. We crossed the parking lot and walked out to the end of the dock. Downriver to our right, a good way in the distance, we could see the I-40 bridge. Upstream and much closer, only a quarter of a mile away, was the Highway 64 bridge. A slight breeze stirred as we leaned against the rail.

"Hey, how come your mom said she was surprised to see me when we got here?" I asked. "Didn't you tell her I was coming with you?"

"Of course not."

"Why not?"

She looked at me as though I should know the answer, which I didn't.

"Um, no offense," she said, which generally meant there would indeed be offense, "but you aren't the most reliable guy these days."

"What are you talking about?"

"There have been plenty of times when you said

you were coming with me but backed out at the last second."

"So?"

"So?" she repeated. "When my mom knows you're coming with me, she always cleans up the guest room and puts freshly washed sheets on the bed for you. I don't want her to be disappointed when you don't show up, so I just quit telling her when you were coming. You know, just in case."

I thought back. Surely I hadn't cancelled out at the last minute more than a time or two. And surely I had a good reason for doing so. I started to argue in my defense, but I figured Sara would spin it to make me the bad guy. Although, the more I thought about it, I did tend to cancel quite often for no reason other than I didn't want to get out of bed.

"Sounds like you have a good system in place," I conceded. It looked like she was about to say something, but I was struck by a thought and interrupted her.

"Oh, you'll never believe what I found out earlier."

"What?"

"Your parents used to think we were dating. Isn't that crazy?" I laughed.

She looked off toward the 64 bridge and brushed a strand of hair from her face, tucking it behind her ear. "Yeah," she agreed, quietly. "Crazy."

"I know, right?"

She turned back to me. "Wait. How did you find out?"

"Your dad told me when you were out running and being all healthy."

She looked confused. "Why would he tell you

that?"

I shrugged. "No idea. Retirement seems to be making him much chattier. He even asked me what the nature of my relationship with you was."

She turned her gaze back to the bridge. "What did you tell him?" she casually asked.

"I told him we were just friends, and that we didn't think of each other in *that* way. You know."

She glanced from the bridge to me and back. "Just friends, huh?"

"Yep," I said. "Although, I realized something when we were talking, something I had never thought of."

She glanced at me again. I was starting to find her behavior a little weird. "And what's that?" she asked.

"Well, I realized that you are my best friend. You know, in the whole world."

After a long silence, I was beginning to wonder what was so interesting about that bridge, because she just kept staring at it. I mean, it was just a bridge. I was about to inquire into her fascination with it, but she turned and started walking away. I guessed that she was ready to head back to the Showtime, but she could have at least checked with me. How rude.

I hurried to catch up, and we walked in silence. When we made it back to the Showtime, the band was taking a break, and everyone had stopped dancing. Some were sitting at the tables and others were milling about, visiting with their friends and neighbors as lively chatter filled the air. An older couple noticed Sara as we made our way over to the table where her parents were sitting and pulled her aside. I continued on, not interested in listening to them go on and on about how

Sara looked so pretty and was so smart and successful. That's how I assumed the conversation would go, since that's exactly how most of them went.

I sat down as another older woman I recognized walked up and started talking to Sara's parents. She asked how Sara was doing and proceeded to go on and on about what a beautiful young lady she was, so smart and lovely, and it all made me want to puke.

Before long, Sara rejoined us, and the band started playing again. Everyone but me and Sara got up to dance. A few songs later, when her parents sat down to take a break, winded from their carousing, Sara leaned in and said something to her mother that I couldn't hear and then headed for the door. Not wanting to listen to any more country songs, I got up and followed her out.

"Where you headed?" I called after her as the door closed behind me.

"Home," she said without looking back.

"Awesome," I said. "I'll join you." I jogged to catch up and fell in beside her.

"Suit yourself."

I was really starting to think something might be bothering her.

"Everything okay?" I asked.

She nodded. "Of course."

Okay then. We continued on in silence until we reached her parent's house. Inside, I plopped down on the couch and rough-housed with Max while Sara fixed a glass of ice water in the kitchen. She then walked out the front door without a word.

Now I was really, *really* starting to think something might be bothering her. I got up and went outside to find her sitting in one of the metal rockers on the porch.

"Okay." I sat down in the other chair. "Are you sure nothing is bothering you? Because it sure seems like something is."

"I'm fine," she insisted.

"Mmm hmm, I see," I said, stroking my chin. "The thing is, though, I'm not sure I believe you." A thought struck me. "Is it this thing with the patient you were telling me about?"

She shook her head. "I don't want to talk about it, okay?"

"Okay," I said, "we won't talk about it."

We sat in silence for a while, but eventually I could no longer take it and had to do something because she was really bringing me down.

"Hey, I know what will cheer you up. There's this pair of jumper cables…"

"Oh dear God," she mumbled.

"…and they walk into a bar."

"Please stop," she groaned, but I saw a hint of a smile touch her lips.

"And the bartender says, 'Hey, buddy, I'll serve you, but you better not start anything'."

I barely held my laughter in as Sara shook her head and sighed.

"You are such a dork," she said as the hint of a smile broadened into a full-blown grin. Satisfied that my task was complete, we sat in easy silence until her parents appeared, walking up the road hand in hand.

Chapter 5

Sunday, May 19th, 2002

I awoke the next morning to the smell of bacon and coffee. I was pretty sure there was no better way to wake up. I grabbed my bag and exited the guest room. In the kitchen, I could hear Sara and her parents talking, which meant the bathroom was free for me to use. I took a quick shower and got dressed, tossed my bag of dirty clothes back into the guest room, and joined everyone in the kitchen.

"Good morning, sleepy head," Sara's mother greeted me. "There's plenty left, just help yourself."

I grabbed a plate and glass from the cabinet, and fished a fork out of the silverware drawer. There were two frying pans sitting on the stove top, one with scrambled eggs and one with bacon. I scraped some of each onto my plate, filled my glass with orange juice, and took a seat at the table.

"Did you sleep well?" asked Mrs. Bartlett.

"That I did," I said. "Like a log. Or a baby, whichever sleeps better."

I started devouring the food in front of me.

"Good Lord," said Mrs. Bartlett. "Slow down. You're going to choke."

"Sorry," I mumbled through a mouthful of food. I was conditioned to eat breakfast at a breakneck pace simply because, no matter how early I set my alarm, I usually realized halfway through my morning routine that I was running late for work and would try to make up time by eating as fast as possible.

I slowed to a more reasonable speed as we made small talk and ate. When we were finished, Sara washed the dishes, and I dried and put them away. Afterwards, I sat on the couch and played with Max while she showered. I also took the opportunity to explain to the Bartletts that my boss, Jeff, was a complete tool.

After Sara returned, we all sat at the kitchen table and played cards for several hours. I was no good at Hearts, but for some strange reason I couldn't quite put my finger on, I always enjoyed it.

As noon approached, Sara and I said our goodbyes to the Bartletts, Sara getting hugs from both and me getting a hug from her mom and a possible broken hand from her father.

"You want me to drive?" I offered as we were about to climb into the car.

"I would rather get there in one piece," Sara responded, so I took my usual place as a passenger.

As we left the small town behind and merged onto I-40, I reached for the radio but had my hand slapped away. I didn't know if it was the constant running or the healthy diet, but Sara's peripheral vision and reaction times were impressive.

I leaned my seat back and got comfortable as we crossed the Arkansas River. A few miles later, I was fast asleep.

****

I slept until Sara slapped me on the arm, jarring me

awake.

"Wake up, we're here," she said, killing the engine.

Through the fog of sleep, I realized we were in the parking lot at our apartments.

I stretched and yawned. "Home sweet home," I mumbled.

We got out, grabbed our bags, and walked across the small lot to the sidewalk in front of my building.

"I think I'll go for a run," Sara said. "You want to come?"

"I greatly admire your persistence," I said, "but God no."

"Okay. See you later."

Inside, I unpacked my bag, started a load of laundry, and spent the rest of the day on the couch watching TV and napping. Somewhere around 10 p.m., as I was contemplating a move from the couch to my bed, my phone dinged, letting me know I had an incoming text message. It was from Sara.

Thanks for going home with me.

Chapter 6

Monday, May 20th, 2002

The day started out in the usual way. I was rushing to get to work, cursing the slow drivers that were causing me to be late, and trying to come up with something witty and suave to say to Amy. When I finally arrived, I had to park farther away from the building than usual, so I started jogging across the lot, but I quickly got winded and slowed to a brisk walk. Maybe going for a run every now and then wouldn't hurt. Then again, maybe it would.

When I entered the IT room, Amy wasn't at her desk.

Great, all that rushing around for nothing.

As I made my way to my cubicle, I saw Amy leaving Jeff's office. He was apparently getting an early start on being a jerk, best as I could tell.

As soon as I sat down, Chip's giant head appeared above my monitor.

"I checked out the job boards this weekend," he said. "It's not good."

"Good morning to you, too. What isn't good?"

"There's practically nothing listed for this area."

"So?" I responded.

"So?" Chip repeated. He seemed a bit flabbergasted, for some reason. "If the layoffs hit, we'll probably have to relocate to find jobs. Do you know how expensive that will be?"

I sensed that the question was rhetorical, so I stayed quiet.

"I have student loans," he continued, "and a car payment. Not to mention I still have seven months left on my lease."

He was getting more worked up than usual, so I figured I should say something to help calm his anxiety.

"Seven months, huh? That sucks."

He ran his hand through his hair, took a deep breath, and let it out. "I don't know what I'll do."

I could see this was going to go on a while unless I put a stop to it. Just as I was about to speak, I saw movement outside my cube. It was Amy.

"Are you all right, Chip?" she said, coming to a stop. She was holding a coffee cup in her hand. "You don't look so good."

Chip nodded. "I'm fine. I didn't get much sleep this weekend."

"Is everything okay?" she asked.

Chip nodded once more. "Yeah. I'm just worried about the layoffs."

She smiled and tilted her head slightly. My God she was hot.

"Don't worry. You're one of the best they have in the department and management knows that. I'm sure that will weigh heavily in your favor."

"Thanks," Chip said, smiling. "That actually makes me feel better."

"No problem," she said and continued on to the kitchen. I started to say hello, but she was already gone. I thought about following to get a cup of coffee of my own and maybe engage in a little small talk, but for some reason I couldn't quite pin down, it seemed like a bad idea.

"I sure hope she's right," Chip said, pulling my attention back.

"I have work to do," I responded.

"Oh, right. Me too. Talk to you later." He sank out of sight.

I pretended to check my email as I casually glanced back toward the kitchen to keep an eye out for Amy. I was hoping to say something charming when she passed back by. Luckily, she was taking her time, which in turn was giving me more time to think of something. As I ran a few lines through my head, I didn't notice Jeff appear in my cubicle doorway.

"How are the servers coming along?" he asked, causing me to practically jump out of my seat. What was it with people always sneaking up on me?

"Sorry. Did I startle you?" he asked.

I shook my head. "Nope."

I didn't think he believed me, but I didn't really care.

"I just wanted to check in with you on the servers. See how things are going."

I gave him a thumbs up. "Going good."

"So, they will be ready to go come Friday?" he asked.

I gave him another thumbs up.

"Are you sure?" he pressed. "I can assign you one of the other guys to help out, if needed."

I wondered what part of thumbs up he didn't understand. I also wondered if he thought I was a total idiot. No one would need that long to set up a few servers.

"No need," I assured him. "They will be ready."

"Good deal. If anything changes, just let me know."

I started to give another thumbs up but decided against it since he was struggling with the gesture. Instead, I responded, "Will do."

He smiled in the direction of the kitchen, and I watched as Amy walked by, smiling back at him. Jeff turned to leave, and I wanted to chuck my stapler at him for causing me to miss an opportunity with her. What a tool.

Since there was nothing I could do about the situation, I buckled down and got to work on the servers. I checked my email for real and found one from the infrastructure team that contained the IP addressing, naming, and storage information I needed. Next, I created NIC teams on each server and assigned them the appropriate IP address. After that, I set the names and joined them to the domain, rebooted, and ran one last check for Windows updates. When everything was satisfactory, I configured the iSCSI connections to the new storage pools that were now online. Once that was completed, there was still a good half hour until lunch, so I stared blankly at my monitor to pass the time. I probably should have checked the logs on the old servers, but I felt like I had already accomplished a good deal of work and there was no need to push it.

When lunchtime finally arrived, I snapped out of my daze and walked to the cafeteria. Sara was already there at our usual table, her lunch bag sitting unopened in front of her as she stared out the window. I placed my order with Marge, filled my cup up at the soda fountain, and walked over and sat down.

"You aren't going to believe what Jeff did this morning," I told her.

Sara continued staring out the window, and I noticed her lunch was untouched.

"Hello?" I waved a hand to get her attention. "Anybody home?"

She looked over at me and grinned. "Hey, how's it going?"

I was about to fill her in on how Jeff ruined a perfect opportunity for me to flirt with Amy that morning, but I hesitated. I sensed something was wrong.

"What's your problem?" I asked.

She sighed. "Nothing."

I started to let it go and continue with my story about how Jeff was a tool, but my keen powers of perception told me not to believe her.

"I don't believe you. What's up?"

She hesitated, then started unpacking her lunch. "I spoke to Dr. Carver this morning," she explained as she pulled the containers from her lunch bag and sat them on the table.

"About what?" I asked.

"About the trial." She looked at the containers but didn't open them. It was just as well, since they were unlikely to contain any comfort food that would lift her seemingly dampened spirits.

"And?" I prompted.

"Things got a little heated. I was frustrated that he wouldn't really listen to my argument for recommending Amelia, so I got a bit angry. I said a few things I shouldn't have."

Marge appeared, sliding my food onto the table in front of me. I hadn't even noticed her approaching because I was taken aback that Sara would get angry with a superior. It was unlike her.

"Holy crap that was quick," I said to Marge.

"You're predictable," she responded. "I had the kitchen go ahead and start getting it ready a little before you walked in."

I was impressed. "You get me, Marge. You really do."

She rolled her eyes and walked away.

"See you at three," I called after her. I looked back at Sara. "So, what happened?"

"He reprimanded me," she said.

"Officially?"

She nodded. "And I've been suspended for two days without pay."

I couldn't believe what I was hearing. I had never known Sara to rock the boat like that. "You've got to be kidding me?"

She shook her head. "I wish I was. I was so stupid to let my emotions get the best of me."

"Now, hold on a minute. If there is anything I know about you, it's that you are the most clear thinking and levelheaded person I have ever known. If you got angry, it must have been for a very good reason."

She glanced up from the table with a strange look on her face. I kept expecting her to say something, but she just looked at me for a few awkward moments before smiling and looking back down at the containers.

"Thanks," she mumbled.

I took a bite of my sandwich and, with a mouth full

of food, said, "This Dr. Carver guy sounds like a real tool. You want me to kick his ass?"

She smiled again and actually laughed. "I appreciate the offer, but no."

"Suit yourself," I said, swallowing my food. I noticed her staring at my sandwich, so I stood up, walked over to the condiment bar, and grabbed a plastic knife and some extra napkins. When I sat back down, I cut the sandwich in two, laid the half that wasn't missing a bite on the napkins, and slid it across the table.

"Here," I said. "Enjoy a meal for once."

She looked from the sandwich to the still unopened containers, and back to the sandwich. She picked it up, hesitated, and took a bite. As she chewed, she closed her eyes. "Oh wow, this is good."

I took a bite of my half. "It's not polite to speak with your mouth full," I reminded her as I chewed.

"I see why you order this all the time," she said, also still chewing.

"They definitely make a mean grilled ham and cheese."

We ate the rest of my sandwich in silence. I offered her a drink of my Dr. Pepper, but she drew the line there.

"Thanks," she said as she packed her untouched containers back into her lunch bag.

"It was just a sandwich," I said. "No need to thank me."

"No, I mean thanks for…you know."

I didn't know, but I told her she was welcome anyway.

"So, when does your suspension start?" I asked.

She looked at her wristwatch. "About two hours ago."

"What? Then why are you still here?"

She shrugged. "I was just…you know."

Again, I didn't know.

"If it was me, I would have been out the door the moment they told me," I said. She just shrugged again.

For the next few minutes, I badgered her for the exact details of what got her suspended, but she declined to tell me. She kept dodging my questions and changing the subject until I eventually gave up trying.

As time ran out on my lunch break, I stood and stretched my back, wishing that the chairs were a little more comfortable.

"I better be getting back," I said.

Sara grabbed her lunch bag and got up. "I guess I'll go home and find something to do."

I started to explain to her that she was completely missing an opportunity to do absolutely nothing for a few days, but I remembered who I was talking to.

I dumped my trash, stacked the empty tray with the others, and walked with Sara to the main entrance.

"So, does your two-day suspension include today?" I asked, stopping next to the glass doors, out of the way of the people coming and going.

"No. So, it's technically two and two thirds days."

"Hmm," I said, contemplating. "I wish I was so lucky."

"Just keep being yourself, and I'm sure it will happen for you one of these days."

****

Back at my desk, I continued prepping the servers by installing the monitoring software and management utilities that the department used on each. I had a few more tasks once those were completed, but I realized things were moving along so well that I could realistically have the servers ready by the end of the day, if I really pushed. I imagined how nice it would be to walk into Jeff's office on my way home and announce that the servers were one hundred percent ready. He had been, after all, doubting my abilities to complete them by Friday. And offering to assign someone to help me? That was insulting. Then again, he was a jerk.

As good as it would have felt to rub his face in it, I opted to coast through the rest of the day. It was only Monday, no need to get carried away. If Jeff didn't think I could complete the servers by Friday, I might as well milk it for all it was worth.

When 3 o'clock rolled around, I shook off the daze of near sleep and headed down to the cafeteria, where I purchased a Twix bar. It was a new week, and I hoped things would return to normal out at the Virgin Mary, but as I approached, the kid was there once again.

"You've got to be kidding me," I muttered under my breath, drawing a look from a passing lady. I returned to the cafeteria and purchased another Twix, vowing to always buy two from that day forward, just to be safe.

When I made it back to the bench, the kid slid over against the arm and I sat down. I handed him the extra candy bar, then opened mine and proceeded to properly enjoy it. I tried to ignore the kid altogether, but I couldn't help but notice he was eating his Twix using the correct procedure. I was slightly impressed that he remembered because kids never remember anything important that you teach them.

"I don't want to pry," I said, "but don't you have a home or something?"

He nodded as he took another bite. We sat in silence for a few minutes, enjoying the perfectness of our candy bars.

"So, how was your weekend?" I asked.

He shrugged.

"Yeah, me too." I paused for a moment. "Actually, I had a pretty good weekend, now that I think about it. Today's not so great, though. I have this boss, Jeff. Don't even get me started on what a jerk he is. Anyway, that's neither here nor there, I just wanted to point it out. The main thing is that my friend got suspended from work for the next two days, which means I have to eat lunch by myself like a total loser. Can you believe that?"

He shook his head no.

"Yeah, me either. I just hope Amy doesn't see."

We finished our bars at almost the same time. I took his empty wrapper and stood up.

"Well, nice talking to you."

He nodded and I turned and headed back inside.

Back at my desk, I double-checked both of the new servers to make sure everything was in order. One would be handed off to the database guy on Thursday for installation of SQL and would be out of my hands for good. I would retain control of the other, which would replace one of our aging domain controllers. Despite being late in the day, I went ahead and ran health checks on our existing domain controller and promoted the new server so that Active Directory would have plenty of time to sync overnight. I would check everything the next morning and, if all went well from there, I would go rub Jeff's face in my awesomeness by the end of the day.

As I worked, I kept an eye out for Amy, but she didn't make any trips to the kitchen.

I was absorbed in my tasks when Chip poked his head over my cubicle wall.

"You still here?" he asked.

I glanced at the clock and saw that it was a few minutes past five. I leaned out and looked around the room, noticing several of my coworkers heading out the door, including Amy. I kicked myself for not paying closer attention to the time. I should have already been gone.

"Not for long," I said as I locked my workstation and stood up. "You working late or something?"

He nodded. "A little. I'm about to make some routing changes. I had to wait until after five because it's going to cause a short interruption. Do you have anything going on with your servers that doesn't need to drop?"

"Nope. I'm all good."

"In that case, I'm going to pull the trigger."

"Good luck," I said as I started for the door. "See you tomorrow."

"See ya." He sank back down into his chair.

I made the long walk out of the building and across the parking lot to my Explorer. Out of habit, I glanced around for Sara's car before catching myself. I hoped she was enjoying her time off, but I knew she likely was not.

The short drive back to my apartment made me regret not leaving work a bit early and beating the rush hour traffic. Not that it was *that* bad, but the increase in idiot drivers was causing my blood pressure to spike.

When I pulled into the lot, I muttered one last curse in general for the other drivers on the road and parked in an empty spot next to Sara's Camry. As I climbed out, I contemplated leaving the keys in the ignition and the door open, hoping that someone was looking to steal a ratty old Explorer, but that lead to another thought. Had I renewed my insurance?

I should probably check on that.

As I walked to my apartment, I pulled out my phone to give Sara a call. It rang several times and went to voicemail. Maybe she was asleep or, more likely, out for a run.

I dropped my things in my apartment and walked down to Sara's building. I knocked on her door a few times and waited, but there was no answer. I walked back around her building, crossed the parking lot, and sat down on a bench next to the walking trail. I watched several runners pass by as well as an older couple that were out walking their dog. I recognized them from the building and nodded as they passed by.

It wasn't long before I saw Sara coming up the trail toward me, running at what looked like a full sprint. She slowed when she saw me and coasted to a stop.

"What are you doing out here?" she asked, out of breath. She bent over and put her hands on her knees for a moment.

"I was just enjoying the day. You?"

"Working out some frustrations," she said. She stood up straight, locked her hands together behind her head, and leaned back slightly, stretching and catching her breath, and for the second time in the last few days,

I couldn't help noticing her running attire, which was very small and very tight. I also couldn't help noticing that her long, toned legs were perfectly tanned and smooth and flawless. And her bare midriff was amazingly...

I shook my head to clear my mind. What was I doing? It was Sara, for crying out loud. Good ol' Sara.

She sat down on the bench beside me, still breathing hard.

"I don't know why you insist on torturing yourself like this," I told her, shaking my head.

"It's therapeutic," she said. "You should try it sometime."

"My therapy takes place on a couch, right where it's supposed to."

She smiled. "So, why are you really out here? I know it's not to enjoy the day."

I shrugged. "I don't know. I guess I just wanted to check on you, see how you were doing."

She seemed slightly surprised as she looked down at the ground.

"Really?" she asked quietly.

"Yep." I nodded. "I know what a goody two-shoes you are. I figured this whole suspension thing might be bothering you."

She closed her eyes and sighed, then looked off down the trail. "I'm not a goody two-shoes," she argued.

I laughed. "Yes, you are."

"I am not," she insisted, sounding a little defensive.

I shrugged. "I don't know, I'm thinking the lady protesteth a bit too much."

She turned and gave me a stern look. "Oh my God,

if you are going to quote Shakespeare, at least get it right."

I laughed as she obviously fought the urge to smile, but she failed and looked away.

After a moment, she sighed. "You are right about one thing, though. It *is* bothering me."

"I knew it," I said, raising both arms in the air in victory. She shook her head and sighed again; her already bad habit seemed to be getting worse.

"So, what's the problem?" I pressed.

She looked at me in disbelief. "Were you not paying attention earlier today? The problem is that Amelia is out of options, and Dr. Carver won't listen to reason. It's like the guy doesn't have a compassionate bone in his entire body. And I get it, you know, you can't get attached to potential candidates, but he could at least go talk to her and get to know her a little before casting her aside." As she spoke, I could hear the frustration and anger rising in her voice. "I mean, she's single and has a young kid who is going to have to watch his mother die within the next few months. Any decent human being would want to try to help in any way they could." She stopped and bit her lip in a way that would have been, in other circumstances, cute.

"Wow. That sucks."

I watched another runner go by—a young and very attractive female runner. Luckily, I realized, if a bit late, that this was not the time to stare after her.

"It's just not fair," Sara continued, looking down at her feet. "If I didn't have to have Dr. Carvers' approval, I would just recommend her for the trial myself."

"Wait a minute," I said, slightly confused. "Why can't you?"

She looked at me like I had forgotten how to speak. "Because he has the final say. He's the clinical research director, and I'm just an assistant. Do you not even know what I do?" she asked.

I tried to look offended. "Of course, I do. I mean, maybe I don't know all of the details, but sure, I know what you do." I paused a second. "But let's say I was explaining it to a friend. What would I tell them?"

She shook her head and sighed. I thought she was going to blow off my question, but she answered it.

"I'm a clinical research assistant, in case you even forgot that part. We shoulder a majority of the responsibility when it comes to finding and interviewing potential participants for a trial. For the ones we do here, we take samples, then collate and analyze the data, and help evaluate any possible implications of the trial's results."

I nodded along to what sounded like a very practiced response, as though everything she was saying matched up to what I already knew.

"It's also my job to be familiar with the trials themselves, otherwise I wouldn't know who was and wasn't a good candidate. I have to get to know the potential candidates to make sure they are a good fit. The trials we run here are small, but other organizations will often reach out to a larger area looking for recruits, so we make recommendations to them. That's the case with the breast cancer trial I've been telling you about."

She paused and wiped at the thin layer of sweat on her brow.

"That's how I met Amelia and got to know her and her son. She's incredible. I can't imagine being in her position, but she is so brave for her son and for her

73

sister, even though she's dealing with..." Her voice broke and she stopped.

It was then that a question crossed my mind. I contemplated keeping it to myself, but, against my better judgement, which wasn't always that great, I felt it needed to be asked.

"It sounds like you've gotten to know her pretty well," I said, laying the groundwork. Sara nodded.

"And it sounds as though you really like her," I continued.

"Yeah, so?"

"So," I took a deep breath and let it out, "*is* she the right candidate for the trial, or do you just wish she was?"

I braced for impact as Sara looked over at me, her face darkening. She opened her mouth to speak but paused and looked away. I remained quiet, not wanting to push my luck.

After several minutes passed without a word, I reached over and put a hand on her shoulder and gently squeezed.

"All right," she said, "maybe she isn't the ideal candidate. But she's close enough that she might get accepted if Dr. Carver would just recommend her, but he wouldn't even talk to her or her doctor. She at least deserves a chance. It's probably the last one she will ever get."

I had no reply to that. I wished there was something I could say or do to help, but I knew it was useless to try. I removed my hand from her shoulder; we sat in silence for several more minutes until I had an idea.

"So, there's this pair of jumper cables," I said.

Sara hung her head and I couldn't tell if she was laughing or crying.

"And they walk into a bar."

"So help me God, I am going to punch you right in the throat," she said, and I was slightly afraid she might. When she raised her head, I was relieved to see she was laughing.

Chapter 7

When I walked into work the next morning, Amy was sitting at her desk, typing away on her keyboard.

"Good morning," I said, as I walked by. She must have been concentrating very hard on her work because she didn't hear me. I contemplated slipping quietly back out the door and re-entering to try again but decided against it. I was confident that the right time would eventually come along for me to charm the crap out of her.

As I passed by Chip's cubicle, he looked up and waved.

"Hey, Eric. Good morning."

"Hey, Chip. How did the routing changes go?" I asked as I passed by and entered my cube.

"Smooth as can be," he said, standing up and peering over the partition as I sat down.

"That's nice." I logged into my workstation and opened a remote session into the new domain controller to make sure the sysvol folder had replicated overnight.

"Have you heard any more on the layoffs?" Chip asked.

I shook my head. "Nope."

"I just wish they would get it over with rather than keeping us in suspense until the migrations are done.

76

I've got to figure out what I am going to do."

I sighed and looked up at him. "Would you quit worrying so much? Jesus. You're gonna have an embolism."

He gave me a confused look. "Embolism?" he asked. "Don't you mean aneurism?"

"Whatever," I groaned. "The point is, you're going to have one. Just relax." I suddenly realized that my lot in life seemed to be to cheer people up. I had been doing a lot of that as of late.

"How are the servers coming along?" he asked, thankfully changing the subject.

"Just fine," I answered.

"Uh oh," he said in hushed tone.

I glanced up to see what the problem was.

"What?" I asked.

"Here comes Jeff." He sank back down and out of sight.

A moment later, Jeff appeared in my cubicle entrance.

"Hey, Eric. How are the servers coming along?" he asked, and I had the thought that if one more person asked about the servers I was going to snap.

"Just fine," I said.

"Good. We've had a somewhat unexpected issue come up. Can you meet me in the conference room in about ten minutes?"

"Sure thing," I agreed.

"Thanks." He smiled and disappeared.

The last thing I had wanted to hear was that something unexpected had come up. Everything was going so well, however, that it made a certain amount of sense something would come along eventually and throw a wrench into the works. I sincerely hoped that whatever it was wouldn't interfere with me rubbing Jeff's face in the fact that I was well ahead of schedule.

"What do you think that's about?" asked Chip, suddenly reappearing and causing me to jump.

"Stop doing that," I said. "Or I'll be the one having an aneurism."

"Sorry. So, what do you think it's about?"

I shrugged. "How should I know?"

"Do you think the layoffs are starting early?" He looked genuinely concerned. He also seemed to be ignoring the fact that I already said I didn't know.

"Probably," I said, hoping to send him running off in a panic so I could finish checking on the servers.

"Oh man, good luck," he offered. I nodded and he sank out of sight. Mission accomplished.

I finished checking the DNS server to make sure it had synced and followed up by glancing at the replication logs. All looked well.

Satisfied, I locked my workstation and headed to the conference room. I smiled at Amy as I passed her desk, but she was still too busy to notice. Jeff must have really been piling the work on her, poor girl.

As I entered the conference room, Jeff was sitting on the far side of the table talking to Wyatt Collin, our database administrator, who sat directly across from him. Wyatt was about my age, maybe even a little younger. Everything about him was pretty average, with the exception of his hair. It was thick and dark and always perfect. I wondered, not for the first time, if it might be a wig. Our jobs required us to collaborate often enough that, even though I didn't know much about him personally, I knew Wyatt was a decent, likable guy who was good at what he did. He was also very easy to work with.

"Thanks for joining us Eric," Jeff greeted me. "Please have a seat."

I plopped down at the head of the table, which felt like the right place to be.

"How are you, Eric?" Wyatt asked.

"Good. You?"

"Doing well, thank you."

Jeff spoke up. "Let's just jump right in, shall we? Here's the deal," he said, looking at me. "Wyatt's wife is pregnant with their third child. We were hoping it wouldn't be coming along until after the move, but, as it turns out, they are inducing labor Friday evening. So, Wyatt is going to be out of touch during the migration this weekend."

I crossed my fingers under the table hoping that Jeff was about to tell me the migration was off until further notice.

"So," he continued, "we need someone to handle the database transfer in his place."

Crap. I didn't like where things were headed.

"We're going to need you to fill in for him. Wyatt tells me you are somewhat familiar with his side of things and would be the ideal candidate."

Great, more work for me. Yay.

"So, what all is that going to entail?" I asked.

"It won't be too bad," Wyatt said. "Basically, I will just need you to run a backup of the existing database at the start of the maintenance window on Friday. It's fairly large, but it shouldn't take more than fifteen or twenty minutes. Then, you'll need to restore it into a new database on the new server. Once that is done, I've got some scripts that will need to be run against the new DB to prep it. Then, just bring it online, attach a client to it, and make sure you can log in. From there, you will just pick back up on what you would already be doing by pushing out the connection changes to the workstations."

"Does that sound like something you would be comfortable handling?" Jeff asked. What a tool.

"Of course," I answered. "Sounds pretty straightforward."

"It is," Wyatt assured me. "And to help out, if you can have the new database server ready by the end of today, I can get SQL installed and configured tomorrow and get the new database created that you will restore into."

"Is that doable?" Jeff asked.

There it was; the opening I had hoped for. I paused a moment and stroked my chin.

"Well, it's already ready…already." I winced at my choice of words, wishing my declaration of how good I was had come out a little smoother. I cut my losses and continued on. "As a matter of fact, both servers are ready to go as of this morning. Well ahead of schedule." *Nice save*, I thought to myself as I watched Jeff's face for the forthcoming look of admiration and amazement.

"Good. I'll leave you two to work out the details. Just yell if you need me for anything." He stood up and walked out. No admiration. No amazement. What a jerk.

"Do you believe that guy?" I asked, pointing a thumb toward the door.

Wyatt only gave me a confused look and said

nothing. I was beginning to think I was the only person who noticed what was going on around me.

"So, where do we go from here?" I asked, moving on past my disappointment.

Wyatt opened a notebook lying on the table in front of him and pulled a pen from his shirt pocket. "I just need remote access into the new database server to start with. Since you have it ready, I'll go ahead and get SQL installed today, then we can get together tomorrow, and I'll give you the scripts and go over the entire process. Will you be free at, say, 10 o'clock?"

"Yep, barring any emergencies, of course. I'll give the DBA group remote access as soon as I get back to my desk and let you know when you can get in."

"Sounds good. What's the server name?"

"SVR-SE-DB002," I said, and he jotted it down in his notebook.

"All right. I'll see you back here tomorrow at ten. If I run into any problems, I'll give you a call."

We stood up, shook hands, and went our separate ways. I crossed the hall and entered the tech room, only to see Amy's empty desk. It was amazing the girl got any work done at all.

I slipped by Chip unnoticed, sat down at my desk, and logged in. Before I could open the new server, my desk phone rang. I knew what was coming.

"IT," I said.

"HERK's down," the familiar voice of one of the ladies in the records office informed me.

"I'm on it," I told her and unceremoniously hung up.

After rebooting the server, I hit the recent button on my phone and dialed the extension at the top of the list.

"It's back up," I said the moment someone picked up.

"Thanks," an overly cheery voice responded. "Will the new stuff you guys are doing this weekend keep this from happening in the future?"

"We'll see," I answered with a non-answer.

"I sure hope so," the voice said. I think her name was Cheryl or Sandra or Megan or something, but it didn't really matter.

"Me, too," I agreed.

"Thanks for getting us back up."

"No problem." I quickly hung up before the conversation dragged on into eternity.

I noticed movement above my monitor and looked up to see Chip staring down at me from his side of the partition.

"So? What was the meeting about?"

I sighed and realized I might be picking up Sara's bad habit.

"They wanted my opinion on who should be laid off first. I recommended you."

"You better be joking," he said, looking uncertain.

"Of course, I'm joking, Chip. They were just piling more work on me for this weekend."

"Oh. That sucks."

I ignored him for a moment as I logged into the new database server to add access for Wyatt. When finished, I typed up an email letting him know it was ready. After hitting the send button, I looked up to see Chip still staring at me. I was hoping he had given up and gone away, but no such luck.

"It's going to be a long weekend, huh?" he said,

pointing out the obvious.

I nodded. Since the migrations only involved server and storage personnel, Chip would get to skip out on the festivities.

"I don't envy you guys," he continued. "Of course, I'll just be sitting around worrying all weekend about whether or not I'll still have a job come Monday."

"You'll still have a job," I assured him again.

"I hope you're right."

"When have I never been right?"

"Good one," he laughed as he sank out of sight.

****

When lunch time rolled around, I waited until most of my coworkers were in the kitchen or had left to go wherever it was they went for lunch before locking my workstation and heading to the cafeteria. I wasn't looking forward to eating alone but, thanks to Sara losing her temper with her boss, I had no choice.

As I ordered my usual, I had an idea.

"Can you make that to-go, Marge?"

She nodded. "Shaking things up today?"

"I like to go off-schedule every now and then."

"What should I tell your girlfriend when she gets here?" she asked. She knew Sara and I were not an item and yet she still referred to Sara as my girlfriend, just to annoy me. I used to get defensive about it, which only made it worse, so I eventually learned to ignore it.

"She won't be joining me today," I answered.

"Oh? She finally come to her senses?"

"Ha ha, very funny," I said.

I took my cup and filled it with Dr. Pepper, grabbed a few napkins, and waited until my order was ready.

When Marge slid the small cardboard box across the counter to me, I thanked her and left, heading out to my sanctuary. As I approached the bench, I half expected to see the kid there, but it was mercifully empty. I sat down and placed my drink and box on the seat beside me to deter anyone from joining me. I popped open the box and began eating, staring up at the Virgin Mary as I chewed.

The day was nice, and I enjoyed my lunch immensely, taking my time and savoring each bite. By the time I was finished, the ambient noise of the traffic passing by on Rogers Avenue was making me sleepy. I thought about lying down on the bench and taking a nap, but I didn't want to be mistaken for a vagrant. I fought to stay awake and thought about ways I could possibly impress Amy, most of which involved money I didn't have. I couldn't help but think life would be so much easier if I were rich.

As the time neared 1 o'clock, I gathered my trash and headed back inside, tossing my empty containers in the can outside the main entrance.

When I reached the tech room, I was too sluggish to be charming, so I slipped by Amy unnoticed and managed to make it to my desk before falling into a coma.

I was awakened sometime later by Chip's voice. I raised my head from my desk and looked up to see his giant head in its usual place above my monitors.

"Shouldn't you be working on the servers?" he asked.

I stretched and yawned, glancing out of my cube to make sure Jeff wasn't around.

"The servers are done," I told him.

Chip looked surprised, although I couldn't imagine why. "Really?" he asked.

"Yes, really," I said, taking offense. "You don't have to sound so shocked."

"Oh, sorry," he muttered. "It's just that, you know…" he trailed off and looked away.

"Is there something I can help you with?" I asked.

"No, just taking a breather. We've got some new gateway services in place now, and I'm getting used to all the new logs and traffic patterns, but I've been looking at them so long today that it's all starting to run together."

"That's very interesting," I said through a yawn, already starting to zone out. "And I would love to hear all about it, but I have work to do."

He once again looked confused. "I thought you said the servers were done."

I nodded. "They are. I've got other stuff to do." That may or may not have been a little white lie, but I believed it was justified.

"I should probably get back to it as well. Although, it may be all for nothing come next week."

"You'll be fine," I said again as he sank out of sight.

I spent the next hour killing time by looking busy, squinting at my monitor in deep concentration whenever anyone passed by my cube. When 3 o'clock rolled around, I was mentally exhausted from the effort.

I locked my workstation and headed to the cafeteria to pick up two Twix bars, hoping the bench would still be empty when I got there but assuming it wouldn't be. After paying, I thanked Marge and told her I would see her tomorrow. I walked down to the lobby and out into a near perfect day, weather-wise.

When I reached the bench, the kid was there. He slid over as I approached. I pulled both candy bars from my pocket and handed one to him as I sat down.

"Every day at 3 p.m.," I said. "You seem to be in a bit of a rut."

He concentrated on opening the Twix and didn't say anything.

"I get it, though," I continued. "I'm a creature of habit myself." I opened my bar and took a bite, once again noticing that the kid was following proper Twix-eating protocol.

"Nice day out, huh?"

He nodded.

"You got big plans for the weekend?"

He shook his head.

"Yeah, me either. I have to work Friday night and Saturday, which sucks. And my boss, Jeff, I think I told you about him, just piled extra work on me, so that should be fun. Oh, and get this; he didn't think I would have the new servers ready on time, but I did. And when I let him know, he didn't even say anything. Can you believe that guy?"

He shrugged.

"Well," I rambled on, taking a bite of Twix, "you have to know him, I guess. But trust me, he's a real piece of work."

As I chewed, I looked around to see if there were any adults nearby, but there were none in sight.

"So, who's supposed to be watching you, anyway?" I asked.

Not surprisingly, he didn't reply. He just kicked at the gravel and chewed his Twix. I could see that any questions requiring more than a yes or no answer weren't going to get me anywhere, so I adjusted accordingly.

"Are you here with your dad?"

He shook his head.

"Here with your mom?"

He nodded. Now we were getting somewhere.

"Is she inside?"

Yes.

"Does she work here?"

No.

"Is she visiting someone here?"

No.

I took another bite of Twix and thought for a moment. If Mom was inside, but she didn't work at the hospital and she wasn't visiting anyone, that didn't leave many options.

"Is she a patient?" I asked.

He nodded.

"So, someone brought you here to visit her?"

He shook his head.

"Well, this is maddening," I whispered under my breath. I finished off the first bar of my Twix as I tried to put the pieces of the puzzle together.

"Okay, so you come here each day with your mom?"

Yes.

"And she's a patient?"

Yes.

"But she doesn't stay overnight?"

No.

That seemed very odd to me. Maybe the kid was confused. There were no patients I could think of that just came in on a daily basis except maybe…

I paused and looked up at the Virgin Mary as a thought hit me. Cancer patients. They come in for treatment and leave. Another thought hit me like a ton of bricks as I remembered what Sara had said. *She's so strong for her son.*

"Is your mother's name Amelia?" I asked.

He nodded.

Well, shit. I sat dumbfounded, staring at the Virgin Mary and having no idea what to say. Finally, I did the only thing I could think of. I handed him the remaining half of my Twix. We sat in silence for the rest of my break and, even though I had lost my appetite, the kid had not. He finished off his Twix along with the extra half I had given him, taking the time to savor each bite. And I was very glad to see that because, judging from what Sara had said, it probably wouldn't be long before his life took a very hard turn.

"See you tomorrow?" I asked as I stood up, taking the wrappers.

He nodded and I left, leaving him sitting alone in the approaching shadow of the Virgin Mary.

****

I had once again managed to look busy until 4:30, when Chip's giant head appeared above my monitors.

"Could you do me a favor?" he asked.

"Nope," I said.

"I need a MAC address tracked down," he continued unabated.

"Fine. What is it?"

"I'll email it to you." He sank out of sight. After a few seconds, an email notification popped up. I opened the message and copied the MAC address as Chip reappeared.

I logged into the DHCP server, opened the manager, and navigated to the current address leases. I sorted the MAC column and ran down the list until I reached the spot where the MAC Chip sent me should have been.

"Nothing active," I announced. "Let me double check the RMM."

I pulled up our in-house monitoring tool and opened the reports section. I chose the hardware report, applied a filter containing the MAC address, and hit submit. After a few seconds, the report came back blank.

"Nothing there either. It's not ours. Nothing that's accounted for, anyway."

"Hmmm," said Chip, his brow furrowing. "Okay, thanks." He sank out of sight, and I prepared myself to ride out the next fifteen minutes before sneaking out early. A few minutes later, I got a new email notification, followed by Chip popping up over my wall.

"Can you check that one?"

I opened the message and went through the same steps with the same results.

"Nothing. So, what's the deal with these?"

Chip rubbed his chin. "I'm catching up on the new logs I was telling you about earlier, and I just happened to notice something that looked like proxy activity. Someone was bypassing the content filters for a few minutes yesterday morning. It was coming from inside the network on that first MAC I sent you. Then, at 12:17 p.m., a different MAC accessed the same proxy. That was the one I sent just now."

"Two rogue devices? That's a little strange."

"Yep," he agreed, nodding. "And they have to be domain joined to pass traffic." He scratched his head and looked around for a minute. "I'm going to keep looking and see what else pops up."

"Good luck," I said as he disappeared.

It was only a few minutes later before another email came in and he reappeared.

"Try that one," he requested.

I once again came up empty.

"No go," I told him as a thought struck me. "Have you looked up the prefix on these?"

"No."

"Hang on," I said as I pulled up a MAC address prefix search page. I grabbed the first six hexadecimal digits from the original MAC that Chip had sent and entered them into the search box. Every hardware vendor on the planet was assigned a six digit hex string that was hard coded into any hardware they made. It was how things stayed organized in the world of digital communication. I clicked the submit button and got a result back.

"Multibyte Media Company," I read out loud, perplexed. "What the hell is that?"

"No idea," said Chip. "What about the other two?"

I ran the second one through.

"Vendor not found," I informed him. I ran the third and got the same result. That usually meant one thing.

"It's gotta be a spoof," I said. "They just got lucky on the first one being legitimate, I bet."

Chip looked worried. "Crap. That's not good."

"Maybe not." I motioned for him to come around. He walked around and stood next to my desk, and I motioned once again for him to lean in close.

"What?" he asked.

I lowered my voice so that only he could hear me. "Since these are likely coming from the same person, and that person is familiar with MAC spoofing and using proxy servers to bypass the filters, it's probably someone in the IT department."

"You're probably right," he agreed.

"Of course, I am," I said, only slightly annoyed. "And it's probably no big deal. My guess is it's one of the guys illegally downloading movies or music or something." I didn't bother pointing out that since they weren't bright enough to use legitimate MACs, it was probably someone up the chain of command. Someone like Jeff.

Chip nodded. "Makes sense."

"We just need to see it in the log right when it happens, rather than a day after the fact. If we can catch it active, we stand a good chance of tying it to an IP and finding out who it is." God, I hoped it was Jeff.

"Sounds good." Chip glanced at his watch. "I'll try to keep an eye on the logs in the morning. I'll let you know if I see something."

"Great." I brought my voice back up to near normal levels. "Now, if you will excuse me, it's quitting time."

"It's ten 'til," said Chip.

I nodded. "Yeah, exactly."

****

After a quick stop at the store to pick up supplies, I waited impatiently in the drive-thru line at McDonald's to pick up something for dinner. The girl working the window was cute, and I think she was flirting with me up until I dropped the change she handed me, then opened my door into the wall while trying to retrieve it. Things pretty much went downhill from there.

Once I had my order and was back on the road, I cursed every driver I could see until I pulled into the parking lot of my apartment. I parked in an open spot next to Sara's car, gathered my bags, and somehow managed to make it to my apartment door without losing anything.

After unpacking the bags and putting everything away, I sat down on the couch with my food and began eating and flipping through channels, finding nothing of interest.

When I was finished eating, I picked up my phone from the coffee table and dialed Sara's number. It rang for a while before going to voicemail. I could only assume she was out running again or doing some other healthy activity, rather than lying on a couch enjoying her suspension. Sometimes, I just didn't understand people.

I got up, threw away my trash, and headed out to the bench beside the trail and sat down. It wasn't long before I saw Sara jogging toward me, wearing the same outfit she had on the previous day and glistening with sweat.

I waved as she approached, just in case she was in some sort of athletic zone and didn't see me. She stopped and joined me on the bench, breathing hard, and I waited for her to catch her breath.

"What are you doing out here?" she finally asked.

"You'll never believe what happened today," I told her. "Our DBA is having a baby this weekend. Well, his wife is but, apparently, he has to be there or something. Anyway, I now have to do his job *and* mine this weekend. Can you believe that?"

"The nerve of that guy," Sara said.

I got the feeling she was being sarcastic.

"So, have you been out here running all day?"

She shook her head. "Just most of it."

"I don't get it."

She shrugged. "It's better than sitting around all day worrying about work and Amelia and feeling entirely helpless."

"That's what TV is for," I said. "It takes your mind off of things."

"I wouldn't know, I don't have one."

At first, I thought I had just misheard her. Then I thought maybe she was joking around, but as she sat there without cracking a smile, I began to think she might be serious.

"You're kidding, right?" I asked.

She shook her head. "No, I don't have a TV."

I was flabbergasted. "No TV?"

"No TV."

I sank back against the bench and crossed my arms, thinking.

"No TV," I said again in amazement. "How did I not know this about you?"

"You never asked. And you never come over to my apartment. How could you know?"

"Is this a recent thing?" I asked.

"Nope. I haven't had one since college."

"Oh dear God," I said. "I don't think we can be friends anymore."

She smiled and rolled her eyes. She knew I was joking, of course. And I was, mostly.

"Oh hey, I met Amelia's son today."

She stared at me for a moment, a confused look on her face. "What do you mean?"

"Actually, I met him last week," I said. "I just didn't know who he was."

"Where did you meet him?" she asked, still looking confused.

"Hogging up my bench, that's where."

The confused look only deepened. "Okay," she said, "you're going to have to start over."

"You know that little alcove with the statue of the Virgin Mary?"

Sara nodded.

"There's a bench there. I go out every day at three on my break and eat a Twix bar."

"That's very unhealthy but go on."

"Well," I continued, ignoring her comment, "I go out one day last week and there's this kid sitting there. He's been there every day at three since. At first, I wasn't thrilled about the whole thing. I mean, that's my time to decompress so I can get through the last part of the day. It's kind of my sanctuary. My one guilty pleasure, you might say. But he's a nice enough kid. Never says a word. I don't even know his name."

"Then how do you know it's Amelia's son?"

I shrugged like it was no big deal. "Because I'm very observant."

She shook her head as though to clear it. "Seriously, how do you know?"

I shrugged again. "I don't know, it just hit me when I was asking him questions. I remembered you saying she had a son. It just seemed to fit so I asked him if his mother's name was Amelia, and he nodded his head yes."

She seemed to accept that explanation over my first one, but I wasn't sure why.

"I feel so bad for him," she said. "And for Amelia's sister."

"What about her husband?" I asked.

She shook her head. "He's not in the picture. He took off when Trevor was born. They've been on their own since."

"That sucks."

"It does," she agreed as she stood up. "I need to go get a shower."

"Yeah, good idea," I said, also standing up. "I mean, I didn't want to say anything, but you kind of stink."

She sighed and I laughed.

We walked from the bench, across the parking lot, to the sidewalk running along the front of the apartment buildings. My building was directly in front of us and Sara's was off to our left. Before going our separate ways, Sara stopped and turned to me.

"I've got my meeting with Dr. Carver Thursday morning. I could really use a distraction tomorrow evening, so I don't go crazy worrying about it." She looked down at her feet. "Do you maybe want to go out and grab a bite to eat or something after work? It would really help take my mind off of things."

"Well, tomorrow *is* Star Trek night, but I guess I could make an exception."

She looked back up and smiled. "Thanks. It would really mean a lot to me."

"Then count me in. See you tomorrow after work."

"See you then," she said and turned away.

She had only made it a few steps before I called after her. "And nothing healthy, you hear me. I want good food."

Chapter 8

Wednesday, May 22nd, 2002

The next morning, after struggling to find the motivation to roll out of bed and go to work, I walked into the tech room only ten minutes late. Amy was at her desk and looked more hot than usual, although I couldn't quite put my finger on why. One thing was for sure; all of the nerds in the place would definitely spend the day drooling over her and vying for her attention. And Jeff would probably be calling her into his office multiple times, using some useless task as an excuse to talk to her, and she would be forced to smile and laugh at his lame attempts at humor while inside she would be cringing at just how....

"Can I help you?"

Amy's voice shook me from my thoughts. I realized I had come to a stop near her desk and was looking directly at her. She appeared to be a bit annoyed, so I assumed that, in the ten minutes of work I had missed so far, she had already been bombarded with multiple, awkward flirting attempts by many of our coworkers.

"Oh, uh, I was just..." I stammered and pointed in the general direction of my cubicle. "I was, uh..."

I kicked myself for not having something charming and funny loaded in the chamber for emergency use. I tried to think quickly but was coming up blank, so I decided to extricate myself from the situation before things got awkward. Without a word, I took off walking to my cubicle. I kept my head down and didn't look back until I was seated at my desk. It was then that I realized why Amy was looking extra hot. It was her blouse. It was cut lower than usual and showed off a fair bit of cleavage, which was great. The part that wasn't so great was that I may have been looking in that general area when she saw me.

This day is off to a good start. I began going through server logs and reports to take my mind off of it.

What felt like an eternity later, but was less than two hours, I stood up and made my way over to the conference room to meet with Wyatt, making sure to keep my eyes on the floor as I passed Amy's desk.

Wyatt, with his unnervingly perfect hair, was already at the conference table and was busy hooking up the projector to his laptop. He glanced up as I walked in.

"Hey, Eric. How are you? Could you grab those lights?"

"Sure," I said, flipping the switches off as I walked by. I took a seat across the table from him as he finished connecting his laptop.

"That should do it." He grabbed the remote lying on the table and turned on the projector. After a few moments, his desktop appeared on the pull-down screen at the front of the room. It was neat and orderly, unlike my own computer desktop.

"Let's start with the SQL server," he suggested. He pulled a piece of paper from a notebook beside his laptop and slid it across the table to me.

"Those are the SA credentials for the new SQL install, as well as an outline of what needs to happen."

I glanced over the paper as Wyatt opened a remote session into the server. I watched as he opened the SQL Enterprise Manager and logged in using the same SA credentials he had given me.

"Okay, here's what we have," he continued. "I've created the new databases here and here. Permissions are all set and ready to go. When you do the restore, just follow the notes I am going to email you. Make sure all of the restore settings are correct, otherwise the collating sequence won't match, and you'll have to redo the whole thing. It's not too big a deal since the restore should only take about half an hour, but I'm sure you would rather get done as soon as possible. I've also got all the settings lined out for the backup of the live database. Those will be in the email as well. Just be sure to take it offline before starting."

I nodded. The SQL backup and restore utility was fairly simple, so I wasn't too worried.

"Now for the important part. Once the restore is done, you need to run some scripts against the databases before you connect any clients. This is the part that is going to take some time."

"How much time?" I asked.

"It's hard to say," he said. "My best guess is probably around an hour on the first one, give or take. After that, there are two more that need to be run. Those are less intensive and should be done in around fifteen minutes each, I would think. All of them are located here, in this folder called 'scripts'. Just pop them open in the editor and execute them in order. Wait until each is done before moving to the next."

I did a quick calculation in my head. An hour total to backup and restore the databases, then somewhere around an hour and a half to run the scripts. While those were running, I should be able to get some of my own tasks done, but I would probably be over an hour behind what I would have been without the extra work. That would put me pushing out the connection scripts for the workstations later than I had hoped. On top of that, I had to migrate the data shares, which was not going to be fun or quick. I had the very real fear that I might still be at work come Monday morning.

"Once those are done, just connect a client and test HERK. I've provided admin credentials for HERK on that sheet of paper, and the email will have a list of things you will need to check and how to check them. It's pretty straightforward."

"And what if they don't check out?" I asked.

"Then you pull the plug," he instructed. "Don't push out the connection strings. We'll stay on the current DB until we figure out why, then try again in a week or so."

I sincerely hoped things checked out because I didn't want to come in on a weekend again anytime soon.

"Any questions?" he asked.

"Nope. I might have some after I see your email, but for now I'm good."

"Good deal." He shut off the projector and unplugged the cables from his laptop. "I'll be available the rest of today and all of tomorrow, but after that I'll be out of pocket for a while."

He grabbed his things, and we both stood up to

leave.

"Thanks for handling this for me," he said as we walked out the door. "Good luck."

"No problem." I tried not to sound too put out. "Good luck on the whole baby thing."

A big, goofy grin spread across his face. "Thanks. This will be our third."

"Yeah, I heard," I said. I couldn't understand why he was so excited about it. I figured one baby would be bad enough, but three was just ridiculous.

We said our goodbyes, and Wyatt turned and left while I took a deep breath to calm myself before entering the tech room. As I walked in, I could see from the corner of my eye that Amy was still at her desk. I summoned every bit of willpower I had to keep from looking at her, but unfortunately it wasn't enough. At least I was able to keep it to a quick glance.

On my way to my cube, I saw Chip staring intently at his monitor.

"Anything on that MAC spoof today?" I asked.

"Oh, hey, Eric," he said, glancing in my direction. "Nothing yet."

I sat down at my desk, logged into my workstation, and proceeded to go through my daily routine of looking busy until something that couldn't wait came along. As lunch time was closing in, I received an email notification. I expected to see a message from Chip, followed by him popping up over my cube wall like a giant whack-a-mole, but the email was from Wyatt. I read through it, getting a feel for the procedures that I would need to run through on Friday night. I decided to check the credentials he supplied me, just to be certain that they worked. I logged into the SQL server first, then HERK, but just as I was about to close out of HERK, I paused.

I leaned out of my cubicle and checked to see if anyone was around. I could see Amy still at her desk up front and two other coworkers standing outside Jeff's office, talking. Luckily, Jeff was nowhere to be seen. I glanced behind me to make sure no one was in the kitchen and might possibly be passing my cube at any moment, but the coast was clear.

Turning my attention back to my screen, I used what little knowledge I had of actually navigating the HERK application to pull up the patient search.

I didn't have much to go by other than a first name, so I typed in 'Amelia' and came up with a surprisingly long list of eighteen patients. It would take too long to open each patient's record and glance through it, so I tried to think of something I could filter on in order to narrow down the results. I thought about checking admitted patients, but since the Amelia I was looking for wasn't technically admitted, I figured it would get me nowhere. I decided to filter on an age range, hoping I could narrow it down to just a few. I chose twenty-five to forty as a starting point and hit the apply button, which shortened the list from eighteen to five. Much better. I took another quick peek around to make sure no one was close by. I opened the first record, looking for any mention of breast cancer. Finding nothing, I moved on to the next record, then the next. Still coming up empty, I opened the next to last record and saw what I was looking for.

Amelia Winslow, age thirty-one. Breast cancer. That had to be her. Up until that moment, I'd known what I was doing could get me into trouble and was a huge violation of privacy, but it didn't truly hit me until I was staring at private medical records. What was I doing? It wasn't like I was going to find a box labeled 'Enter patient into drug trial' that I could simply check and be done with it. And even if there was, surely someone would notice the change, wonder what had happened, and change it back. Or worse, track it down to the login that Wyatt had given me.

I closed out of HERK and bided my time until lunch.

****

When I walked into the cafeteria, I was surprised to see Sara sitting at our usual table. Rather than order my food first, I walked over and sat down.

"What are you doing here?" I asked. "I thought your meeting was tomorrow."

"It is," she said. "I just needed to get out for a while so, against my better judgement, I thought I would come meet you for lunch."

"What if I had a lunch date with Amy or something? This could have been awkward."

She rolled her eyes. "I figured I would take my chances."

"Oh, speaking of Amy," I said, slapping the table. "You should see her today. She has on this low-cut top that is so hot, I'm surprised it doesn't burst into flames."

Sara stared silently at me with a blank expression. Perhaps she didn't hear me or fully grasp the hotness I was attempting to describe, so I tried again.

"It's cut down to about here," I explained, pointing out the approximate spot on my own chest. "And it's awesome."

If that didn't properly explain it, I didn't know what would.

Sara closed her eyes, took a deep breath, and let it out slowly.

"Is this what we are going to talk about?" she asked, opening her eyes.

It was definitely what I wanted to talk about, but I sensed that maybe Sara didn't.

"I tell you what. I'm going to go order some food. While I'm gone, if you can think of something better to talk about, if that's even possible, then we'll talk about that."

"That shouldn't be a problem," she said as I stood up and walked over to the counter.

I waited in the short line and as soon as I reached Marge, she went in back for a moment and reappeared with my usual.

"How did you know?" I asked, feigning excitement.

"Just give me your money," she said.

I handed her a twenty and told her to keep the change for being so awesome.

After filling my drink at the fountain, I sat back down and noticed for the first time that the table was empty in front of Sara.

"Are you not going to eat?" I asked.

She shook her head. "I'm not hungry. I'm too nervous about tomorrow."

"Why?"

She looked at me with a funny expression. "Oh, I don't know, maybe because I might lose my job. Or my chances of ever getting a promotion may be gone. Or Dr. Carver could just make my life miserable until I can't take it anymore and quit."

I took a bite of my sandwich and thought a moment. "Why is everyone around here so worried about losing their job? Between you and Chip, it's all I hear." I paused to swallow. "I mean, it's just a job."

"Maybe for you," Sara said, looking far too serious. "For me, it's more than that. I love what I do. It's a chance to help people and maybe even make a difference every now and then. It's not just a job to me."

I took a moment to think again. "I still don't get it." Before she could reply, I held my sandwich out in front of her nose. "Are you sure you don't want at least a little?"

She leaned back and made a face. "Do you mind? I told you, I'm too nervous to eat. I'd probably just throw it all back up."

"Gross." I pulled the sandwich back and took a big bite.

"By the way," I mumbled through the mouthful of food, "I have admin access into the database through the weekend. If you want me to bump up your pay or anything, just let me know."

"That may be a moot point come tomorrow," she said. "And why on earth would anyone give you access to anything of importance?"

I shrugged. "Beats me. I also have an admin login to HERK. I looked up Amelia Winslow's record earlier when no one was watching."

Sara looked astonished. "Why on earth would you do that? That's a huge privacy violation," she said, mirroring my own thoughts from earlier. "Couldn't that get you into serious trouble?"

I nodded and took another bite. "Oh yeah, it definitely could."

"Then why do it?" she asked.

I shrugged again. "I don't know."

"You don't know?"

"I don't know," I repeated slowly, then took another bite of my sandwich. "I guess maybe I was hoping there was something I could change in her records to get her into that trial you've been blabbing about."

Sara rubbed her eyes with the palms of her hands and looked at me like I had grown a third eye. "You've got to be kidding me."

I paused as I realized that telling her what I had done was turning out to be a bad move. I shrugged yet again. "I don't know what to tell you. I just thought it was worth checking."

She shook her head in disbelief. "It doesn't even work that way. There are forms that have to be filled out, signatures..." She paused, momentarily at a loss for words, for which I was grateful, but it was only a few seconds before she found her voice again. "You are an idiot."

"You shouldn't be so timid and reserved," I said. "You should tell people how you really feel."

She leaned forward and slowly and softly banged her head on the table. I continued eating as I watched her.

Finally, she raised up and looked around the room. "I should have stayed at my apartment," she mumbled. "But no. Go meet Eric for lunch, I thought. It'll do you some good, I thought."

I swallowed a mouthful of food and finished off

my Dr. Pepper.

"Now who's the idiot?" I asked with a smile.

We spent the rest of the lunch break engaging in idle chitchat, not touching on anything important. The only exception was when I tried once more to explain how hot Amy was looking that day, but Sara just sighed and changed the subject. I had a few minutes left before I needed to get back to work, so I walked with Sara out to her car. As we stepped outside, the sky was clear and the sun was beating down on the asphalt, but the weather had yet to turn uncomfortably hot.

"Are we still on for dinner this evening?" she asked.

"Yep," I answered. "What are you going to do until then to keep from worrying about tomorrow?"

"I need to pick up a few things from the store. Then I might read a book or go for a run," she said.

I should have guessed that last one.

"Well, that all sounds lovely."

She grinned, which I was glad to see. When we reached her Camry, she pulled out her key and hit the button to unlock it. "What time do you want to meet?"

"How about 6 o'clock?" I suggested as I stepped in front of her and pulled the door open.

"That sounds good," she agreed. She sat down in the driver seat and, once she was situated, looked up and said, "Thanks again. This really means a lot to me."

"It better. I'm missing Star Trek for this." I shut the door before she could respond. Through the window, I watched her smile and shake her head. I took a step back as she started the car and drove away.

****

When I arrived back at the tech room, I glanced in

Amy's direction as I passed by her desk. I somehow managed to trip over my own feet but, luckily, I stayed upright. I heard a nearby laugh but I didn't stop to see who it was. Instead, I silently cursed the entire room and kept going as though nothing had happened.

I spent the next two hours alternating between doing nothing, fighting to stay awake, and going over the procedures that Wyatt had sent, just to be certain I had no questions before he disappeared for the week.

At 3 p.m., I picked up two Twix bars from the cafeteria and headed outside to my sanctuary. I was slightly disappointed when I saw that the bench was empty. I sat down and held my Twix in my hand, turning it over and over but not opening it yet. Maybe the kid was just running late. If so, I didn't want to get started without him and wind up having to watch him enjoy his Twix while mine was already gone.

Five minutes later, I couldn't wait anymore. I tore open the package and started eating, still expecting the kid to show up at any minute.

When I took the last bite, I realized he probably wasn't going to appear.

Oh well, more Twix for me.

I pulled the second bar from my pocket and held it in my hand, but as I started to open it, I paused, hit by a sudden, unnerving thought. What if something happened to Amelia? Maybe that's why the kid wasn't there.

I shook away the thought and stuffed the Twix bar back into my pocket.

It's probably melted by now anyway, I thought as I stood up and headed back inside. As I entered the main lobby, I turned, without thinking, away from my normal path up to the tech room. I knew where I was headed, but I kept my mind blank for some reason I wasn't quite sure of. I simply kept walking.

When I reached the cancer treatment section, I headed straight through the small lobby and toward the treatment rooms, as though I was supposed to be there. I passed through a set of double doors and into a hallway that was lined on both sides with rooms. A nurse, standing next to a desk just ahead, looked up from her paperwork. I walked over to her, said hello, and told her I was from IT as she glanced at my badge.

"We're trying to update some of our asset records," I told her. "Do you mind if take a quick look at the workstations you guys have in this area?"

"Help yourself," she said with a smile. "You can start here if you want." She gestured to the workstation sitting on the desk.

At that moment, I really wished I had brought a notepad with me so I could pretend to write things down. I quickly formulated another plan as I stepped around the desk. I bent over the workstation and opened the command prompt, typed in 'ipconfig /all' and hit enter, and hoped that the information scrolling up the screen would look impressive to the nurse.

I stood up straight and stroked my chin in thought as I nodded to myself and closed the command prompt.

"Thanks," I said. "I just need to take a quick look at the rest."

I walked down the hall and peeked into the first room. It was empty, but I entered anyway to keep up appearances. I went through the same exercise on the computer just in case the nurse passed by. When it felt like I had been there a sufficient amount of time, I walked back into the hallway and down to the next room, which was also empty.

I once again opened the command prompt, typed in a command, and looked at it with the proper amount of concentration, just in case. After a few seconds, I closed the prompt and crossed the hall and was about to enter another room when movement farther down caught my eye. It was the kid. He had appeared from the room two doors down from where I was. I ducked inside the room in front of me before he looked my way. Thankfully, the room was empty. I stood close to the door and peeked out into the hall. The kid was walking toward me with his head down. I stepped to the side of the doorway and flattened myself against the wall so he wouldn't see me as he walked by. I waited a few moments before risking another glance outside. I saw him at the desk, saying something to the nurse, but they were too far away for me to hear what was being said.

The nurse smiled at him, and they both started walking toward me. I stepped back, out of sight, and waited for them to pass. When I looked out again, I saw them disappear into the room two doors down, where the kid had come from.

From what I could tell, the kid had not looked distraught in any way. In fact, he looked like he always did; face blank and staring at the ground. That seemed like a good indicator that nothing horrible had happened.

I moved quickly to the next room and slipped inside, hoping it would be empty like the previous one, but prepared to act nonchalant if it wasn't. For once, luck seemed to be on my side. I stayed in the room, standing at the workstation with the command prompt open, waiting on the nurse to pass back by. I could hear muffled voices coming from the room next door but couldn't make out anything. Before long, the nurse passed back by, stopping in the doorway when she saw me.

"How's it going?" she asked.

"Almost done," I said, and she moved on.

I took a deep breath and let it out. I knew I should just call it good and leave. I had, after all, seen the kid and he appeared to be fine, which likely meant his mother was also still fine. Well, maybe not fine, but alive at least.

Against my better judgment, I exited the room I was in, walked straight to the next one, and entered without hesitating.

As soon as I was inside, I stopped. The room was much larger than the first three I had been in and was filled with two rows of recliners that looked very comfortable. Between each of the recliners was a small table, much like a nightstand. Windows along the back wall let in plenty of sunlight that made the room feel open and fresh. In the front row, sitting in one of the chairs with her feet propped up was a woman who appeared to be my age, if not younger. She wore a white robe and hospital gown and had her right arm laid out straight on the chair's armrest. A tube ran from her arm to a machine behind her. She smiled at me and I smiled back and, despite having a thin cloth hat covering her head, I could tell she was completely bald.

Sitting in the next chair over was the kid. He looked up at me and waved.

"Oh, hey." I waved back. "How's it going?"

He shrugged and looked down at the floor.

I turned my attention back to his mother. "Sorry to bother you. I'm with IT. I just need to check a few things on the computer over there." I pointed to the workstation that sat along the wall to my right.

"Check away," she said, cheerily. Maybe it was her smile or something more subtle, or maybe it was the fact that I knew a bit of her story, but for some reason I couldn't quite grasp, I immediately liked her.

I walked over to the computer and ran the same command, following it with the ping command for added flair.

I waited a few more moments before closing the prompts and heading for the door.

"Oh really," the woman was saying as I walked by. She looked up at me with a stern face, stopping me in my tracks. "Have you been giving my son candy?"

I froze, unsure what to say or do as my heart started pounding.

I stammered, trying to explain the situation, but I stopped trying when her face softened, and she started laughing.

"It's fine. I'm just messing with you."

I exhaled, realizing I had been holding my breath. "Good one," I said. "You had me there for a minute."

"Although," she continued, "I'm wondering if I should be concerned that the IT guy is passing out candy to children."

"It's in my job description," I said. "I'm not sure why."

"Your job description, huh?" she asked, grinning.

I nodded. "I thought it was weird, too."

I felt I should introduce myself, although I wasn't sure why.

"I'm Eric," I said.

"Nice to meet you, Eric. I'm Amelia." Her smile was warm, and I realized that, if you threw some hair back on her head, she would be very pretty.

Before I could catch myself, I said, "I know."

She looked slightly perplexed. "You do?"

I needed to change the subject very quickly. I thought for a second and remembered the Twix that was still in my pocket.

"Speaking of candy," I said, pulling the bar out, "I'm down to the last one for the day. Is it okay?" I nodded in the kid's direction.

"Sure," she said with a smile.

I handed the bar over to the kid, who took it eagerly and began tearing into the package.

Amelia glanced at the candy wrapper. "Twix, huh? You guys give out the good stuff here."

"Only the best," I said. "Are you a Twix fan?"

"Oh, of course. I don't trust anybody who isn't."

I laughed. "I knew there was something I liked about you."

After getting the package open, the kid held out one of the bars to his mother.

"No thanks," she told him. "I'm nauseated as it is. Any food will push me over the edge." She reached across the small table with her free arm and gently squeezed the kid's elbow. He smiled at her and began eating as I felt something mushy and sappy inside of me trying to make its way out. I forcefully stomped it back down.

Amelia looked from Trevor to me, still smiling, and said, "I guess I should at least ask how you two know each other since you aren't a doctor or a nurse, and I haven't seen you in here before. I don't want to look like a bad parent by not checking."

"No offense, but your kid takes candy from strangers, so I think the bad parenting ship has already sailed."

She laughed at that, and it made me like her even more, but I did feel compelled to explain things.

I told her about the bench and the Virgin Mary statue and how it was my sanctuary and Trevor had taken it over and I had no choice but to give him his own Twix to keep his focus off of mine. She laughed a few times throughout.

When I was done, she looked over at Trevor. "I'm going to have to have a talk with Natalie about letting you run around outside by yourself." She turned to me. "Natalie is my sister. She's usually here with me, but she had to run some errands after she dropped me off. And she usually keeps an eye on this little guy, although I'm now finding out it's not a close eye." She turned her attention back to Trevor. "So, do you go out there every day just for the free candy?"

When I look back on that moment, I know she was just asking it jokingly and not expecting an answer, but Trevor's reply sucked all the air out of the room. It was the first full sentence I ever heard him speak.

"I go there to pray that you'll get better."

I felt like I had been punched straight in the heart. Tears welled in Amelia's eyes as she took Trevor's hand, and I suddenly felt like an intruder of the worst kind.

"I should probably get going. It was nice meeting you."

Amelia glanced at me and nodded as a tear rolled

down her cheek.

I left in a daze. On the way out, I think I may have told the nurse that I was finished with the computers, but I'm not certain.

As I walked, I could feel something in the pit of my stomach and could only assume that the sandwich I had for lunch must have been bad. I would have to speak with Marge about that.

I didn't pay attention to where I was going; I just wandered the hallways, one connecting to another and another, until I rounded a corner and ran headlong into someone.

"Sorry," I said, looking up to see a doctor, white lab coat and all, standing in front of me. His hair was silver; though he didn't look overly old, he did look angry.

"Watch where you are going," he barked.

I glanced down at the nameplate on his coat.

J. Carver.

I realized I was near the labs where Sara worked and that this was her superior. The same one that had reprimanded and suspended her. I also realized that it would have been unfortunate if he had become a surgeon with a name like Carver.

He reached out and held my badge between his thumb and pointer finger and read it.

"Well, Eric," he said as he let it go, "are you just going to stand there like a simpleton or are you going to move?"

As quickly as I had liked Amelia, it was nothing compared to the speed and degree to which I disliked Dr. Carver.

"Sorry," I said again, and stepped to the side. I felt

like I needed to explain why I was there. I also felt like I needed to punch him square in the neck, but instead, I quickly pulled a reason for my presence out of the air. "I was told there was a printing issue over here so I—"

"I don't care," he interrupted. "Check with Carrie." He brushed roughly past me, and I watched in utter amazement as he disappeared around the corner.

"Wow, what a jerk," I observed out loud. I looked around to make sure no one heard me, although I'm sure if anyone had, they would have agreed.

Rather than checking with Carrie as Dr. Asshat had so kindly recommended, I turned and headed in the general direction of the tech room. My break was long over, and I hoped no one had noticed me missing.

****

When I walked back into the tech room, I assumed I would be bombarded with questions as to my whereabouts for the past forty-five minutes, but no one seemed to notice. I sat down and tried to clear my head, but nothing was working. The only thing I could do was sit there visualizing my foot connecting with Dr. Carver's ass and wishing for 5 p.m. to arrive.

Around 4:30, Chip appeared above my monitor.

"Hey, Eric," he said. He looked tired. "How's it going?"

"It's going great," I answered, but I think the sarcasm might have been lost on him.

"Have you heard anything else about the layoffs?" he asked.

I sighed and rubbed my temples. "No. I haven't heard anything. Would you give it a rest already?"

"Sorry. The waiting is driving me nuts."

I knew I needed a diversion to get him off of the

layoffs, or else I might go nuts as well. "Have you come up with anything new on those MAC spoofs?"

He shook his head. "Nothing."

"Well, maybe whoever it was realized we were on to them. Either that or they finished downloading—"

"Hey, guys."

I almost jumped out of my seat but quickly tried to recover and act normal as I realized it was Amy's voice that had interrupted me.

"Hey, Amy," Chip said.

I looked over to see her standing outside my cube. It took extraordinary effort to not look at her blouse, but I somehow managed to meet her eyes. "Hi, Amy."

"Jeff's inviting everyone to Ed Walker's after work for a pre-migration get-together. It's sort of a thank you for everyone who has to work this weekend. Can you guys make it?"

I opened my mouth to speak but Chip beat me to it.

"I'm not a part of the migration. Does that rule me out?"

Amy smiled and it was glorious. "Of course not, Chip. You're always invited." She turned to me and I quickly met her eyes because mine had drifted a little south.

"What about you? Can you make it?"

And there it was: the moment I had been imagining for a long, long time. Amy had just asked me out. Okay, maybe it wasn't *exactly* as I had imagined it, but it would do. And technically she was asking everyone out, but I still counted it as a win.

"Yeah, I would love to." I winced inside as I heard the words come out of my mouth. *I would love to? I sound like a blushing schoolgirl. What the hell is wrong with me?*

"Great. We're all going to meet there right after work."

"Awesome," Chip said as Amy smiled at him and walked away. He looked down at me and whispered, "It will be like the last supper before we all get canned."

Or something like that. I wasn't really listening too closely. I was busy trying to remain calm inside because I was going to get to hang out with Amy outside of work. How great was that? Granted, Jeff was going to be there, that jerk, but I was willing to take what I could get. I began imagining a group conversation slowly leading to a conversation between just Amy and me. Then, as the evening was wrapping up and everyone else had left and it was just me and her, she would invite me back to her place and...

A shiver ran through my entire body.

"Uh, are you okay?"

I looked up to see Chip still hovering over me.

"Yes," I said, maybe a little defensively. "Don't you have some logs to watch or something?"

He made a funny face. "You're weird sometimes," he said as he sank out of sight.

"*You're* weird sometimes," I mumbled.

I spent the next fifteen minutes or so catching up on emails and creating a checklist of the migration tasks I would be responsible for. When I finished, it was 4:45 and it felt strange to not be planning my exit. As I was trying to figure out what to do with my hands to look busy until 5 o'clock, I remembered something—my dinner plans with Sara.

"Shit," I whispered out loud as I suddenly found myself in a bit of a pickle. I certainly didn't want to let

Sara down, but, at the same time, I might not get another opportunity with Amy.

I tried to figure out what to do in a rational and intelligent manner. On one hand was Sara, who was worried about her meeting in the morning. On the other hand was Amy and her cleavage. I was faced with a monumentally tough decision.

Out of the blue, a simple solution hit me. I would text Sara to explain the situation and let her know I needed to push our dinner back to seven instead of six. Unless, of course, things went as I had earlier imagined, in which case I would have to postpone dinner indefinitely. I was sure Sara would understand. After all, she knew my feelings for Amy. She would probably be happy for me and would tell me to go ahead and have fun and not worry about meeting her at all, that she would make do. Yes, of course that was how it would go because Sara was the greatest. She would undoubtedly understand.

I fished my phone out of my top desk drawer; before I could start a message, Chip sprang into sight.

"I've got a hit," he announced excitedly.

I knew what he was talking about, so I shushed him. "Keep it down. If it's one of the guys in here, you're going to scare them away."

"Oh, right," he said, his voice almost a whisper.

"Email the MAC to me," I said as he sank out of sight. I tossed my phone back in the drawer and waited on Chip's email. A few seconds later, the new message notification dinged. I copied the MAC from the message, opened the RMM, and initiated a hardware inventory sync. While that was running, I opened a command prompt, pinged our network broadcast address and waited for it to time out. Once that was done, I entered 'arp -a > eric.txt' and waited until the cursor reappeared. I then pulled up the notepad application and opened the eric.txt file that had been created. Inside was a complete list of every device on the network, along with each associated IP and MAC address. I hit the search button, pasted the MAC address Chip had sent and got a match.

The MAC tied to an IP address of 10.150.10.178.

"Bingo," I said quietly as Chip reappeared above my monitor.

"Did you find it?" he asked.

I held up a finger, switched back to the RMM, and waited for the sync to finish. After roughly thirty seconds, it was done. I opened the devices list and filtered on the IP that I had found in the ARP output. One device popped up named W003-04-2. I clicked on it to view its details.

The RMM listed everything about the computer, including RAM, hard drive usage, processor, and every other thing anyone would ever want to know, but I was only interested in one piece of information, which was the currently logged in user. I scanned down through the list until I found it and was surprised by what I saw.

SEHjcarver.

"What the..."

"Did you find it?" Chip asked again.

"Hang on." I wanted to be sure of what I had found, so I switched back to the command prompt and entered 'nbtstat -a 10.150.10.178' and hit enter. The MAC address that Chip had sent was returned as expected. Next, I entered 'nslookup 10.150.10.178' and hit enter, which returned the PC name W003-04-2. It all matched up.

I leaned back in my chair and stared at the screen, thinking.

"What is it?" Chip asked again. I looked around and could see my coworkers starting to gather their things. It was five o'clock and I certainly didn't want to be the last one to the restaurant, because every other nerd in this place would by vying for a seat close to Amy. If I was late, I would be left out in the cold. I wasn't about to let that happen.

"I'm not sure yet," I answered. I typed out a quick email to James, our antivirus guy, asking if computer W003-04-2 had reported any malware as of late. After hitting send, I locked my workstation and grabbed my keys from beside my monitor. People were already filing out of the room. There was no time to waste.

"What do you mean you're not sure yet?" Chip asked.

"Exactly that," I said. "I'm not sure yet. I'll do some more digging and let you know something tomorrow." I walked briskly away, filled with a sense of urgency.

"Hey, wait up," I heard Chip say from behind me, but there was no way I was going to be slowed down.

I casually followed my coworkers out of the building, wanting nothing more than to shove them aside and sprint to my Explorer, then drive like a bat out of hell to the restaurant, where I would grab a cozy booth in the corner and wait for Amy to arrive. As she entered, I would catch her attention and point to the empty seat across from me. She would join me, and the rest of the story would one day be told to our grandkids. Censored, of course.

Instead, I held myself back until we reached the parking lot. Everyone started dispersing to their vehicles. At that point, I walked briskly to mine, hoping not to break a sweat in the process.

When I reached my Explorer, I hopped in and cranked the engine. There was a moment of panic as it sluggishly turned over, followed by relief as it churned to life.

With little to no regard for my fellow drivers, I navigated expertly up Rogers Avenue until it joined Towson. I took a left, only slightly running a red light, but it wasn't my fault. The yellow had been way too short. I made a mental note to write the mayor a sternly worded letter about the traffic signals in town.

I made my way briskly up Towson, where I topped the small hill in front of the other hospital in town, and descended the other side. At the bottom sat Ed Walker's Drive In, famous for their French dip sandwiches.

I had been there plenty of times, but I had never had the French dip sandwich, primarily because they served a mean grilled ham and cheese. It was even better than the hospital cafeteria's.

I pulled into an empty spot and killed the engine. Through the dirt on my windshield, I could see that I was the first one to arrive. My plan was falling nicely into place.

I went inside and was greeted by a familiar waitress whose name I could not remember.

"Have a seat anywhere you like," she said.

Ed Walker's had started out in ancient times, somewhere in the 1940s. It began as a gas station, then somehow progressed into a burger joint. The building itself was small and looked like it was frozen in the

1950s. Old Coca-Cola signs, records, and photos hung on the walls. The counter just inside the front door was lined with barstools and trimmed in chrome, with the kitchen located behind it. Off to the right, a narrow aisle ran along the front of the building, lined on each side with tables and booths. Toward the end, two small rooms that had been added over the years connected off to the left to provide additional seating.

I grabbed the last booth, just outside the rooms, and sat down facing the doorway. The entire front wall of the building was windows, so I watched for my coworkers to arrive as the waitress took my drink order.

It wasn't long before I saw Amy climb out of the passenger seat of a brand new, extended cab Ford F-150, which I recognized immediately. My stomach churned in disgust as Jeff appeared from the driver side, along with two other coworkers that climbed out from the back seats. Other cars were pulling into the lot as well, but I paid them no attention.

I waited patiently as everyone gathered in the lot, then started toward the front door.

Jeff, being a complete jerk, held the door open for Amy and the others, as though they weren't capable of something as simple as opening a door.

As the group made their way down the aisle, I saw Chip's giant head at the back of the group, peering around them. He saw me and waved. I looked in panic from him to Amy, to Amy's cleavage, and back to him. If I didn't act fast, he would likely ruin my plan by wanting to sit with me and, not being the smallest guy in the world, leave no room for Amy.

"Hey, Eric," Jeff said as they approached. "You didn't waste any time getting here."

What a jerk.

He took a seat in the booth two up from where I sat, and Amy joined him before I ever had the chance to catch her attention. The booth between us filled up, as well as the one across the aisle. Bringing up the rear, Chip plopped down across from me in my booth.

"I'm starving," he announced.

I lowered my head to the table.

After a few moments, I somehow found the strength to sit up and make small talk with Chip until the waitress came to take our orders, at which point Jeff stood up.

"Dinner's on me, everyone," he said. "Enjoy."

His grandstanding in front of Amy and everyone else was enough to make me nauseated, but not so much that I didn't order the most expensive thing on the menu.

When the food arrived, I looked at my steak and sighed, wishing it was a burger or, better yet, a grilled ham and cheese. Jeff had got me again. What an ass.

I ate begrudgingly and halfway listened to Chip complain about layoffs and the job market and other things I didn't care about.

Everyone around us chattered and laughed and seemed to be having a good time. I tried to listen in on any conversations coming from Amy's table, but it was just far enough away that I couldn't make out anything being said.

"I sure hope it turns out to be nothing," Chip said, pulling my attention back to our booth.

"What?"

"The proxy access and MAC spoof. I hope it's just malware or something. Hey, maybe I should check with

James to see if he's had any malware activity lately. Maybe we can match something up."

I shook my head. "I already sent him an email, just before we left."

"Oh, cool." He took a bite of his burger and looked around at everyone as he chewed. I followed his gaze and watched as people laughed and talked.

"I sure hope this isn't the last time we are all together," Chip whispered.

There were eleven of us in all, counting me and Chip, and, on the surface, I considered almost everyone to be annoying. As I thought more about it, though, I started realizing that maybe they weren't all that bad and if I never got to work with them again, I would maybe, just a little tiny bit, miss them. I could certainly do much worse when it came to coworkers. And these were all good people, as far as I could tell.

Except for Jeff, of course. He was the worst.

"Same here," I agreed.

As dinner wound down, Jeff stood up and got everyone's attention to do more grandstanding.

"I just want to say thanks to you guys. Even though not all of you will be working on the migration this weekend, I still wanted to treat everyone to dinner and let you guys, and girls," he glanced over at Amy and smiled, "know just how much I appreciate you all and how great it is working with you. We make a great team." He paused and raised his glass. "Here's to us."

Everyone raised their glasses in response and phrases like "here, here" and "thanks for dinner" were tossed liberally about. Even though I thought they were all idiots for falling for Jeff's sappy gesture, I couldn't help but grin a little and raise my own glass.

As Jeff sat back down, Chip turned to me, leaned in, and whispered, "I've got a bad feeling about this. That sounded like he knows something that we don't."

As paranoid as Chip was, I realized he might be right.

A little later, someone decided it was time to go, and everyone followed. I watched forlornly from my seat as Amy stood up and headed out with the group. I sighed and stood up along with Chip and moped my way outside. Everyone gathered in a loose group, once again thanking Jeff for dinner and saying their goodnights. I hung around so as not to appear ungrateful but was glad as people started going their separate ways.

Jeff and his three passengers were parked close to me. I was doing my best not to look at Amy as I walked by until Jeff caught my attention.

"Thanks for coming, Eric," he said.

I nodded. "Sure thing."

"And thanks especially for covering for Wyatt this weekend. Did you guys get everything lined out?"

"Yep."

"Good deal. See you tomorrow." He climbed into his nice, new truck along with the others.

I walked over to my rundown Explorer and sighed before opening the door. I climbed in and watched Jeff pull away. I could see Amy's silhouette in the passenger window.

I sat there for a moment, trying not to think about much of anything. Soon, the moment stretched out to several, until I finally decided to head home. It was then that I remembered Sara. I hadn't texted her yet to let her know I would be late.

"Shit," I said out loud and reached for my phone, but it wasn't in my pocket. I looked over to the passenger seat to see if I had left it lying there, but the seat was empty. Maybe I had left it on the table. Just as I was about to climb back out, it hit me. I had been in such a hurry to leave, I had left it in my desk drawer.

I smacked the steering wheel. "Shit, shit, shit."

I started the engine and thought for a moment. The clock on my dash showed 7:03 p.m. The sun was hanging low in the sky, but there was still some daylight left. Should I go straight to the apartment, or should I swing by work and grab my phone first? From where I was, the hospital wasn't on the way, but it wasn't terribly far out of the way either.

I took a left onto Towson and decided to go back for my phone first. I was already an hour late, what was another twenty minutes? I was sure Sara would understand.

As I traveled back up Towson and onto Rogers, traffic was lighter than it had been earlier, so I made decent time. When I pulled into the parking lot at St. Edwards, I was hoping to get a closer spot than usual but had no such luck.

As I walked across the lot, I noticed Jeff's empty truck. After dropping off Amy and his other passengers, he must have gone back inside. I fantasized about keying it as I walked past but kept my hands to myself. It was the thought that counted.

The IT department ran a skeleton crew overnight that consisted of only two guys manning the help desk. They worked out of a smaller office next door, so the tech room was empty when I walked in. Only the lights in the front of the room were on, but they cast enough light back to my cubicle that I could just see where I was going. I grabbed my phone from the desk drawer and was about to hit the wake button when I heard muffled laughter. I paused and waited until I heard it again. It sounded like Amy. And it sounded like it was coming from Jeff's office. I was about to walk toward it when I heard the rattle of his doorknob. I'm not sure why I did it, but I quickly ducked into my cube, out of sight.

"Behave yourself," I heard Jeff say, followed by a short laugh.

"What if I don't want to behave?" Amy said.

"Then I'll have to reprimand you."

That was just like Jeff, using his authority to threaten his subordinates. What a jerk.

"Oh?" Amy said. She sounded as though she were laughing off his threat. It struck me as a little odd, but maybe that's how she dealt with things, by trying to defuse the situation and make light of it.

I was tempted to walk right up there and give Jeff a piece of my mind, but before I could move, Amy spoke again in a conspiratorial voice.

"Hey, let's go back in your office and, um, have a little fun. What do you say?"

"I would love to," Jeff told her. "Believe me I would, but it's too risky. We could get into serious trouble if anyone found out about us."

"Aw, come on. Pretty please."

I realized I had quit breathing. I stood up in the darkness and started walking toward them.

"No can do," Jeff insisted. "How about we just go back…"

He stopped talking when he saw me approaching.

Amy followed his gaze over to me and they both took a step back from each other.

"Hey, guys," I said.

"Oh—hey, Eric," Jeff stammered, clearly caught off-guard. "You startled me. When did you get here?"

I held up my phone. "I forgot this."

He smiled nervously. "I see."

We all three stood silently, looking back and forth at each other until Jeff spoke again.

"I just had a few things to wrap up," he explained. "Amy here was kind enough to lend a hand."

I looked over at Amy. "How nice of you," I said, quietly.

She smiled awkwardly but didn't say anything back.

I looked back to Jeff. "Have a good night." I turned away before he could respond.

I don't remember the walk to my car, all I knew is that by the time I got there, I was angry. Very, very angry. I sat alone, gripping the wheel, and staring straight ahead. Time stretched out, but I couldn't move. The sun set, and the sky turned orange. It might have been beautiful for all I knew, but at that moment I had no use for sunsets or beauty. I just wanted all the lights to burn out so I could be alone in the dark.

****

Eventually, I drove back to my apartment. In a daze, I had somehow managed to start the engine, shift into gear, and begin moving. I squinted into the glare of oncoming headlights as I drove slower than I had ever driven in my life, until I pulled into the parking lot and parked next to Sara.

I sat there a moment before looking at my phone

for the first time. There were three missed calls and voicemails, all from Sara. I also had three texts from her. I pulled up the first one.

Hello? You're late, which shouldn't surprise me. Where are you?

I always marveled at the way she insisted on using proper sentence structure in her texts. She was quite possibly the only person on the planet who did that.

I moved on to the second text.

Me again. Where are you? You better not have forgotten about dinner ;)

The last message was sent just after 8 p.m.

Okay, I'm getting worried. Where are you? Please call or text me.

I looked at the time and was surprised to see that it was almost 8:45. Dinner with Sara was definitely out of the question. I was sure she had already eaten without me, and since I had already eaten as well, I could see no reason to extend the already long day. I felt worn out and beaten down. I was tired mentally and physically.

I climbed slowly out of my vehicle and trudged to my apartment. Inside, I collapsed onto the couch without turning the lights on and sent Sara a text.

sry. something came up. will explain ltr. going to bed

A minute later, I got a message back.

Can we talk in the morning? Before work?

I typed out a reply.

yep

I set my phone to vibrate, leaned over, and fell asleep.

Chapter 9

Thursday, May 23rd, 2002

I awoke from a dream where I was punching Jeff in the face over and over, my fist making a thumping sound each time it made contact. I stretched and yawned, my back stiff from sleeping on the couch, and heard the thumping sound again even though I was awake.

It took me a moment to realize someone was knocking on my door. I checked the time and saw that it was 7:35 a.m. I stood up, still fully dressed, shoes and all, stumbled my way across the small living room, and pulled the door open to see Sara standing there with a concerned look on her face.

"What happened?" she asked.

"Hmm?" I responded, still sluggish from just waking. "Oh, you mean last night?"

"Yes."

"The guys from work got together for dinner at Ed Walker's. It was sort of a pre-migration thing to get ready for the weekend or something like that."

She looked confused. "You got together with 'the guys' for dinner?"

I nodded.

She looked even more confused. "But *we* had plans for dinner."

"True, but this came up at the last minute."

"I don't understand. You don't even like your coworkers."

"Also true," I agreed, stepping outside and closing the door. I wasn't sure why at the time, but I had never invited her into my apartment in the three years I had lived there. I guess I didn't want her to see that I was a bit of a slob.

"So, you just went anyway, despite having plans with me?" she pressed. She seemed to be growing a bit agitated. I knew I needed to properly explain.

"Only because Amy was there," I added, satisfied that would cover it.

Sara opened her mouth to talk but nothing came out.

"I was going to text you," I continued, "to tell you I was going to be late, but I left my phone at work." That's when the incident in the tech room came flooding back into memory.

"Get this," I said, as Sara's mouth still moved wordlessly. I was worried for a split second that she might be having a stroke or something, but I moved on. "When I went back to get my phone, I accidentally overheard Jeff and Amy. They were in his office." I took a deep breath and let it out. "I think they are having an affair." Saying the words out loud made it seem all too real. I cringed inside.

"Unbelievable," Sara whispered. She appeared to be as angry about it as I was. She turned and started walking toward the parking lot, so I followed behind her.

"I know. I mean, it's Jeff for crying out loud. Why would anyone in their right mind want—"

Sara stopped and spun around. "How could you?"

I stopped in my tracks, a bit confused. "How could I what?"

Her eyes widened. "Are you serious?" she almost yelled. "You've got to be kidding me." She turned and started walking again.

"What?" I said, following and starting to feel a bit agitated myself.

She spun again. "We had plans, Eric. You knew I was worried about this meeting I'm about to have." She turned again and I followed.

"I know. But it was Amy. It was my chance to get close to her."

As we reached her car, Sara spun around again, and I was startled by the look of anger on her face.

"Jesus Christ, Eric! When are you going to get it through your thick head that she doesn't like you?"

I flinched noticeably. "What are you talking about?" I could feel my own anger start to rise.

"I was counting on you to be there for me." She turned and reached for the car door.

"Wait a minute. What do you mean she doesn't like me?"

"I mean she doesn't like you," she repeated herself, her voice raised.

"How would you know?" I fired back, my voice raising as well.

"Because she told me," Sara yelled.

It was my turn to move my mouth without finding any words.

Sara lowered her voice a bit. "She told me, okay?"

My thoughts were a jumble, and I was getting angrier by the second, but I managed to say, "You don't even know her. How is that possible?"

"I ran into her at the supermarket a while back." She paused to shake her head. "I don't have time for this right now. I have a meeting to find out if I get to keep my job or not."

"Wait," I demanded, my anger still building. "Why would she just tell you in the supermarket that she doesn't like me?"

"Look," Sara said, "she doesn't like you. Get over it."

"You know what I think?" I countered. "I think you're just jealous."

"Jealous?" she fired back. "Of what?"

"That she's prettier than you."

Sara froze and I froze. I didn't know why I said it because it actually wasn't true. Maybe it was just being told Amy didn't like me, piled on top of finding out about her and Jeff, that made me want to lash out. Whatever the case, I said it.

Sara stared at me, and her eyes glistened with tears.

"I have to go." She flung the car door open.

"Sara, wait." I took a step in her direction, but she sat down and slammed the door closed, started the car, and took off, tires squealing. I looked around to see if anyone was watching, but there wasn't another soul to be seen.

As I walked back to my apartment, I tried to tell myself that I had done nothing wrong, that Sara was just overreacting. By the end of the day she would be calm and rational, and all would be well.

****

I had very little time to get ready for work. I showered at a record pace, not really bothering with all the details, brushed my teeth in hectic fashion, and managed to get my clothes on in the right order.

I grabbed my phone, keys, and ID badge, and headed out the door.

The drive over to the hospital was brutal. I hit every light and traffic was not cooperating in the least. I was growing angrier and angrier at everything around me.

When I reached the tech room, I walked quickly past Amy without even looking her way and plopped down at my desk. No sooner had I hit the seat, Chip's head appeared.

"I got another hit earlier this morning," he confided.

"I don't care," I snapped.

"Geez, what's wrong with you?"

I took a deep breath and calmed myself. "Sorry. It's just been a bad morning."

"Is everything okay?" he asked.

Every fiber of my being wanted to point out the fact that his question was ridiculous. Anyone could plainly see that everything was not okay. Chip was so oblivious sometimes it made me want to scream.

"Just send me the MAC," I said as I focused on my monitor.

He sank out of sight, and I logged in to the network. I opened my email and noticed I had a new message from James, the endpoint security guy. It was a reply to my message late yesterday. I read through it, but there was nothing to report. There had been no detections on a PC named W003-04-2 anytime recently.

Oh well, I thought as Chip's email arrived. It was probably malware that was flying under the radar, or maybe a backdoor allowing someone to access the system. Or, and I stopped to consider more carefully, maybe Dr. Asshat was up to something. How likely was it that a jerk like him was smart enough to attempt to conceal his activity while using a proxy to bypass the content filters? Probably not very, but it might be worth exploring. Whatever the case, someone needed to track down what was being accessed through the proxy. That would usually fall to a combination of people, including James, but something told me to hold off before passing it off to them.

Chip mercifully left me alone for the next few minutes as I ran through the process of trying to find the IP associated with the new MAC. Unfortunately, I came up empty.

"Find anything?" Chip asked, reappearing above my monitor and startling me.

"Stop doing that. I swear to God, I am going to mace you one of these days."

"Sorry," he said. "Wait, you have mace in there?"

"No, I don't have mace in here. It's just a figure of... Look, just quit sneaking up on me like that."

"I'll try to do better," he said earnestly. "So, did you find anything?"

I shook my head. "Not this time. How long ago was the hit?"

"About forty minutes now."

"That would probably explain it. They most likely got what they were after and switched the MAC back."

Chip grinned. "MAC back. That sounds funny. It rhymes."

I closed my eyes and sighed. "Dear God, Chip."

I opened my eyes to see his grin widen. "What? It's

funny."

"I've got work to do," I said, hoping he would take the hint. "Let me know if you get any more hits."

"Will do," he responded. "There probably won't be any during the day, though. I've noticed they only happen at the beginning or end of the day, with the exception of one at noon. Most of them are just outside of normal day shift hours." He sank out of sight.

That's interesting. Although, it did make a certain amount of sense. If someone was doing something they shouldn't be doing, they wouldn't do it when other people are around. They would come in a little early, or stay a little late, switch their MAC address and route through the proxy, do whatever it was they were doing, then switch it back. It had the makings of someone being very careful, but not a master hacker. At least, not that I could tell. It was just someone who knew a little but certainly didn't cover all their tracks.

I realized I was probably missing the obvious. If I were going to do something that was against company policy, I wouldn't use my own computer.

I pulled up the RMM audit logs and ran a search on Dr. Carver's PC. I searched through for any remote sessions into his computer but found none. After that, I used the RRM to pull the security log from the PC itself and began searching it for any unusual sessions. After several minutes, I had come up empty. Either someone really knew what they were doing, or I was back to my original thought.

Another obvious scenario struck me. Someone could have figured out Dr. Asshat's password. He, like many users, probably kept it written down on a sticky note under his keyboard. And, knowing him, it was probably 'iamajerk123'. Anyway, someone was likely using his login, which was the obvious explanation for not seeing any other user activity in the logs. I kicked myself for not thinking of that first.

I pulled up the company directory and dialed Dr. Carver's extension but got no answer. I followed by dialing the extension of someone named Carrie, who worked in the same department. The name sounded familiar to me. Maybe Sara had mentioned it once.

A pleasant female voice answered the phone.

"Hi," I said, "can you tell me if Dr. Carver is available? I just tried his extension but didn't get an answer."

"I'm sorry, he's in a meeting at the moment. Can I take a message?"

I slapped my forehead. Of course, the meeting with Sara. I wondered how it was going.

"This is Eric with IT," I explained, "we've had a few problems with the domain controller over here and, well, I won't bore you with the details, but the end result is that you guys will need to change your passwords right away or you will get locked out of the system."

"Oh, okay. How do we do that?" she asked.

"It's easy." I walked her through the process on her PC. "Can you do me a huge favor and make sure Dr. Carver gets his changed as soon as he's out of his meeting?"

"Sure, no problem," she assured me.

"Great. I really appreciate it. Oh, and one more thing. Would you tell everyone to be sure to log out of their PCs at the end of their shifts? I know it's company policy to never leave a PC unattended while logged in, but I also know it's easy to forget that. Could you just give everyone a reminder?"

"Of course. We're usually very good about that around here."

"Awesome," I said. "Thank you for all of your help."

I hung up and sat back in my chair to think. If someone was using Dr. Carver's login, and they were using it just before he came in or after he left for the day, that should thwart their next attempt. If everyone did what they were supposed to, the password would be changed, and the PC would be logged off. If the hits continued, it would be reasonable to assume it was Dr. Carver himself.

Satisfied with myself, I started my usual daily responsibilities, but it wasn't long before another thought struck me.

"Hey, Chip," I said loud enough that he would hear me.

He popped up over the cubicle wall in his usual place above my monitors.

"Did you find something?" he asked.

I shook my head. "No, but I had a thought. Doesn't the content filter block known proxy sites?"

He nodded. "Yeah, but this guy isn't using anything known."

"Why not block the public IP that he is using?" I asked.

"I did," he said, "but it keeps changing."

"Have you found where it was coming from?"

He nodded again. "It's always from a block owned by Cox. If it was foreign or anything like that, I would just block the entire range, or add the country of origin

Kevin Johnson

to the geo filter."

I nodded. I should have known Chip had covered those bases. He was good at what he did.

"Okay, just checking."

"No problem. Let me know if you think of anything else." He started to sink out of sight but paused. "Hey, are you in a bad mood today because you heard something about the layoffs?"

"Oh my God, Chip, go away," I said, a little too loud.

He sank out of sight as I wondered what the going price on mace was.

****

When lunch rolled around, I headed to the cafeteria. On my way out of the tech room, I noticed Amy looking in my direction. She smiled and gave a small wave, but I purposely snubbed her.

Doesn't like me, my ass.

When I walked into the cafeteria, I glanced over at our usual table, hoping to see Sara sitting there with her containers of healthy food, but the table was empty.

I spent the rest of lunch break eating in solitude. As I kept noticing the empty chair across from me, I kept thinking about Sara. Maybe I had, in some way, let her down. That, of course, did not give her the right to make things up about Amy.

As I thought about it, I noticed that thinking of Amy did not illicit the warm fuzzy feeling that it used to.

****

I spent the afternoon double checking my lists for the migration and trying to look busy. I let a few of my usual tasks go, rationalizing that they could wait until tomorrow or next week.

Just as Chip had thought, there were no more MAC hits, so there was nothing to take my mind off of things.

I was grateful when 3 o'clock finally rolled around.

I arrived at the bench with two Twix bars in hand to find the kid had returned. I sat down beside him and handed him one of the bars. He took it and waited on me.

"So, how's your day going?" I asked as I opened my bar.

He shrugged and began tearing into his, all while kicking at the gravel.

"Same here." I took a bite. "Same here."

We ate our bars in silence, which I realized was way easier for him than it usually was for me.

"How's your mom?" I finally asked.

He shrugged again.

"You're not much for small talk, are you?"

He shook his head no. I chuckled and sat silently for a while, until I could no longer take it.

"You know, Trevor is a pretty cool name, but I think you need an awesome nickname. What do you say?"

He shrugged.

"How about T-Bone?" I asked.

He smiled but shook his head no.

"Really? That seems like a pretty good one to me."

Another shake of the head.

"Okay, then, but I can't promise I'm going to come up with anything better than that."

I was surprised when he quietly spoke.

"My mom calls me Trev."

In that moment, I felt as bad for the kid as I ever

had for anyone, I think.

"Trev," I said, pretending to think it over. "I like it. That's definitely way better than T-Bone."

He smiled and nodded, still looking down at the ground.

"Your mom seems like she's pretty darned cool," I added.

He nodded emphatically, his smile widening.

We finished our bars in silence and, as my break ran out, I stood and took his wrapper.

"See you around, Trev," I said.

"Bye," he responded.

As I walked away, I couldn't help but notice that my Twix bar hadn't tasted nearly as good as it used to.

****

At 5 o'clock, Chip and I stayed behind as the tech room emptied. We wanted to see if any new hits showed up in the firewall logs, but none did. We gave up at 5:20 and left.

As I exited the lobby, I noticed that the sky was overcast.

"Hey, Eric, wait up." It was Amy's voice, coming from behind me.

I slowed until she caught up.

"How's it going?" she asked.

"Fine," I lied. "You?"

"Good," she said. "Actually, there's something I wanted to talk to you about."

"Oh?"

"Yeah," she continued. "Last night, after dinner. In the tech room. I'm not sure what you overheard, but you might be wondering if there is something going on with me and Jeff."

"I'm not wondering," I assured her.

"Oh." She seemed surprised. "Well, good then, because there really isn't anything, you know, worth mentioning to anyone or—"

"I'm not wondering because I *know* there's something going on," I interrupted.

"Oh." She dropped her tone. "I see."

She fell behind slightly then caught back up to me.

"Listen, I was hoping that we could, you know, maybe keep this just between us. It would mean a lot to me."

We reached my Explorer and I noticed a second ding had appeared on the door. What a shitty week it was turning out to be.

"What do you say?" she asked. "It would really mean a lot to us. We could both get into trouble since he's my boss and everything. He could even get fired over something like this."

"You don't say?" I replied.

She nodded. "So," she said, dragging the word out. "Can we maybe keep this between us for now? Just until Jeff and I figure things out."

I pretended to think for a moment. While doing so, I realized that, up until then, I would have been thrilled to be talking to her alone. I would have been putty in her hands and done anything she asked. Instead, I felt nothing but disappointment. I knew I would never look at her the same way again.

"We'll see how it goes." I climbed into the Explorer and drove away, leaving her standing there with her mouth hanging open.

****

I drove to my apartment under the gloomy sky,

only getting mildly peeved at the traffic around me. When I pulled into the lot, Sara's Camry was there. There was an open spot two spaces down, so I parked there and killed the engine.

After dropping my phone, badge, and wallet in my apartment, I walked over to Sara's building and knocked on her door. I waited and knocked several more times before giving up and heading back to drown my sorrows in whatever soda I could find. I wasn't much for alcohol, which was probably for the best at that moment.

I sat down on the couch and stared blankly at the walls for a good long time. I eventually picked up my phone and sent Sara a text message.

Can we talk?

I waited, staring at the screen for what felt like half an hour, but no reply came. Just as I was about to get up and find something to eat, there was a knock at my door. I opened it to see Sara standing there with her arms crossed, dressed in her usual running attire. I noticed she wasn't sweating as I stepped outside and pulled the door closed behind me.

"Look, I just…"

"Shut up," she said, rather harshly. "Just shut up and listen." She half turned from me so that we were standing side by side, looking out onto the parking lot and the walking trail beyond.

"You don't deserve to know the whole story, but here it is anyway. A while back, I had looked up Amy in the employee directory. I just wanted to see this girl you were always going on and on about. That's all." She paused for a moment before continuing. "A few weeks later, I was at the supermarket. When I got in line, I recognized her in front of me. I don't know why, but I struck up a conversation with her. I told her I thought I recognized her from the hospital and that I worked there as well. I mentioned knowing a guy in IT named Eric. For some stupid reason, I asked her what she thought of you. She just shrugged and said you were okay."

I waited patiently as she paused again. I sensed there was more coming.

"I got the feeling she was just being nice," Sara continued. "I convinced her she could be honest with me. I even told her I thought you were super annoying, just as a show of good faith."

Super annoying? I felt like that wasn't entirely accurate. Occasionally annoying, maybe, but not super.

"That's when she told me she thought you were super annoying as well. She went on to say that you were weird, and you creeped her out most of the time. She said she didn't like having to interact with you."

The words came as no surprise even though, after our fight that morning, I had halfheartedly tried to convince myself that Sara was making up the fact that Amy didn't like me. Somewhere in the back of my mind, however, I knew she had been telling the truth. That, unfortunately, didn't make it any easier to hear the whole story.

Still looking out across the parking lot, she continued, "I never told you because I didn't want to hurt you." She let out a short, sharp laugh. "The ironic part of it is, if I had told you, maybe you would have been there for me last night instead of chasing after her."

"Sara, look, I'm…"

"No," she said sharply. "Don't."

"Please," I pressed on, "I just want to—"

"Shut up," she almost screamed. "You don't get to say anything to me." She turned to face me, and I could see that she was on the verge of crying. "I was counting on you last night, and you let me down. You weren't there when I needed a friend more than anything in the world." She was angry and I couldn't blame her one bit. "I'm going to lose my job," she blurted out.

"What?" I asked, completely shocked. "How?"

"The meeting was a train wreck," she began, turning away again as a tear rolled down her cheek. "I wasn't exactly at my best this morning after our fight. And, with Amelia and everything, I let my anger get the best of me again and..." She shook her head and wiped at her eyes. "I got suspended indefinitely, pending a review next week. I'm certain Dr. Carver is going to fire me."

I couldn't believe what I was hearing. Sara was the most dedicated, caring person I knew. How could anyone want to fire her for being passionate about her job and about a patient? It didn't make much sense to me, but, then again, not a lot did lately. One thing was for sure, though; I had screwed up on a gloriously epic scale. As big of an asshole as Dr. Carver was, I was light years ahead of him in that department. I had let down the best person and best friend I had ever known. I felt like I was going to throw up all over my shoes.

"Sara," I managed to say, "I'm am so—"

"Don't you dare say it," she said, her voice cracking. "Don't even dare."

She wiped at her eyes again and literally ran away from me, across the parking lot, onto the trail, and out of sight under the darkening sky.

****

I spent the next hour sitting on my couch in the growing darkness until I couldn't stand it anymore. I had to get up and do something, anything. I went outside into the warm night where I could smell a hint of rain in the air. I could hear a faint buzz coming from the two streetlights that illuminated the front half of the parking lot and the sidewalks in front of the apartment buildings. Just beyond the darkened back half of the lot, the lampposts along the running trail cast pools of light at intervals. In one of those pools, the bench sat empty.

I started walking toward it, past my run-down Explorer sitting among much nicer cars, including Sara's Camry. I reached out and laid a finger on it as I passed by.

I sat down on the bench just as a lady walking her dog strolled by. The dog trotted over to me, pulling against its leash, and I put my hand down to pet it. He jumped up, putting his paws on my knees.

"Bobo," the lady said. "Be good." She looked at me with a kind smile. "Sorry about that." She pulled him back toward her.

"No worries." I tried my best to smile.

She moved on, and I sat there for a while, wondering what to do with the rest of the night, until movement down the trail to my right caught my eye and I saw Sara running along at a brisk pace. I was surprised she was still out here this late and this long. She must have logged quite a few miles. I was even more surprised when she stopped and sat down.

I didn't risk saying anything right away. I simply took what I could get.

As we sat in silence, a light mist began to fall, creating a halo around the orange glow of the lamp post lights. I held my hands out, palms up and could barely feel it at all. Sara sat there, unmoving. Either she hadn't noticed it yet, or she didn't care.

As the seconds extended out, I finally had to say something to break the silence and to attempt to ease my own, troubled conscience.

"I'm sorry, Sara."

I didn't expect any kind of reply, so I was surprised when she answered back.

"You should be."

I deserved that. And much worse.

"I wish I could go back in time and change everything," I continued. "I really do."

She laughed, just a short snort of air from her nose. "Well, you can't."

And that was it; the best I could do. Sitting there in the light mist, next to Sara, I felt like the world's worst human being. I wanted to properly explain everything to her, to let her know just how sorry I was, but there was something fundamentally broken in my ability to do so. I realized it was a flaw that I had been carrying with me my whole life but had been blissfully unaware of until that moment. Suddenly it was front and center, illuminated with a light that burned brighter than a thousand suns, with flashing signs pointing at it whose marquees read, "You suck, you really do." I was truly afraid I would never be able to tell her how I felt.

Despite my shortcomings, I started to speak again, if only to fill the void between us, but Sara stood up and walked away before I could say a word.

I watched as she moved away from the lamppost

light and became only a silhouette as she crossed the parking lot and reappeared under the streetlights. She followed the sidewalk to her building, and I continued watching as she disappeared around the corner.

I sat there on that bench, staring at the corner of the building, hoping she would return but knowing she wouldn't. Why would she? But still I kept looking, even as the rain turned from a fine mist to something more substantial, then to a downpour.

Chapter 10

Friday, May 24th, 2002

The next morning, I awoke early without an alarm clock. Since we would be working late into the night and possibly well into daylight the next day, those of us doing the migration were allowed to come in at noon. But I was up early because I was determined to set things right. I hadn't slept well, but I wasn't tired. I was full of nervous energy and anxiety.

I fixed breakfast and swallowed it, almost whole. After taking a shower and getting dressed, I marched down to Sara's apartment and knocked on the door, entirely unsure of what, exactly, I was going to say.

After waiting the appropriate amount of time for an answer, I knocked again, a little louder. Still, there was no answer. I knocked again.

"I'm not leaving until you open the door," I called loudly, hoping Sara could hear me. Still there was no answer. It was just past 7:30, and I wondered if she was already up and out for a run. Just to be safe, I knocked again, even harder.

The door to the apartment next to Sara's opened and a large man wearing sweatpants and a white t-shirt stepped out.

"Knock it off, asshole. Some of us are trying to sleep."

"My apologies," I said, and, for some reason, I bowed in his direction. He gave me a look that said I was the biggest moron he had ever seen in his life before going back inside.

I waited for a few more moments before giving up and crossing the lot to sit on the bench, hoping Sara would be coming along at some point, but she never did.

Two hours later, as the sun was starting to beat down on me, I went back inside and sat on the couch, stared at the walls until 11 o'clock, then fixed myself a sandwich and mentally prepared for a long day and night.

****

I walked into the tech room a few minutes before noon, ignoring Amy as I passed by her. I stopped outside of Chip's cubicle, where he sat bent over his keyboard, focused on the monitor in front of him.

"Anything this morning?" I asked.

He jumped slightly and looked over at me. "Oh, hey, Eric. You snuck up on me there," he said, and I felt a slight tinge of satisfaction.

"Sorry about that," I told him, even though I most definitely wasn't. After all, turnabout was fair play, as they say.

"No problem," he said. "Nothing at all today."

I nodded. "Okay. Keep me updated."

I stepped around to my cube and sat down to think for a moment. Either the password change had worked and locked out whatever third party had access to Dr. Carver's PC, or the good doctor himself wasn't feeling up to doing anything shady that morning. Of course, another possibility was that the third party was also laying low and hadn't tried to log in yet.

Whatever the case, I realized that I was no closer to figuring out what was going on than I had been the previous day. I needed another hit to show up before I could start eliminating options.

I sighed, grateful for the momentary distraction, and logged into my workstation to begin my daily routine. When I was done, I once again went through my task list for that night. You never knew what might go wrong, but I felt pretty confident that I had all the bases covered. With any luck, I would be in bed before sunrise.

At 2:30, I received an email from Jeff calling for a meeting of everyone involved in the migration for 3 p.m. in the conference room.

Just great. Leave it to Jeff to throw off my entire routine on a day as important as this. What a jerk.

At 3 o'clock, I made my way begrudgingly to the conference room. The migration team consisted of five people. There were two guys from the application development team, Jerry and Thomas, who worked on customizing HERK and a few peripheral applications that interacted with it. There was also Paul, from the storage side, and the two young helpdesk guys, Jimmy and Pat, who wouldn't be doing any of the real work, but would be there to help out with any PC issues that might arise.

Oh, and there was Jeff, who also wouldn't be doing any real work, so he didn't count.

After a few minutes of small talk, Jeff asked for everyone's attention.

"Okay, guys," he said, "I just wanted to get everyone together really quick to run through the overview one last time and field any questions." He glanced at me and quickly looked away. "The maintenance window is set for 5 p.m., but we won't start until 5:20, just to give any stragglers time to wrap up what they are doing. If you don't mind, let's each run through our high-level plan for everyone else's benefit, including mine."

He pointed to me. "You should probably start us off, Eric. And by the way, Eric is filling in for Wyatt as well, so thank you for that."

"Sure." I cleared my throat. "I'll be mirroring all data from the old array to the new. I've already had that running, so it's mostly up-to-date. I'll run it again at 4:00, then do one last refresh at 5:20. I'll also start the database backup at that point, then move it over and restore into the new SQL server. Then I'll be jumping back and forth between running Wyatt's scripts on the DB to prep it, configuring the new shares, and enabling the new GPOs to remap user drives to the new array. Somewhere in there, I will demote the old DC. When the database scripts are done, and if all is well, I'll let Jerry and Thomas know. I'll also let Paul know that we are finished with the old array. Then I'll push out the new connection strings for HERK to the workstations and let Jimmy and Pat know if there are any issues so they can chase them down. And that's pretty much it."

"Thanks," said Jeff without looking at me. He pointed to Jerry and Thomas.

It was Thomas who took the lead. "We'll be working on a few things with peripheral applications until we hear from Eric. At that point, we'll connect them up to the new DB and start testing. Then we'll go home early while the rest of you poor souls continue on."

Jeff pointed to Jimmy and Pat.

"Um, we'll just be sitting around waiting on someone to tell us what to do," Pat told him. Everyone but me chuckled.

Paul chimed in. "I'll handle any changes with the new array if needed, but mostly just wait for the all clear, at which point I will take the old array offline so there is no chance of anyone accessing the wrong data come morning. Oh, and Ryan from infrastructure will be on call in case there are any routing or switching issues."

"All right," Jeff said, standing up. "It sounds like we're ready. Keep in mind that the drop-dead time is 3 a.m. If everything isn't stable at that point, we have to start the roll back in order to return to a functional state by 7:00. I know it's going to be a long night for everyone except Jerry and Thomas, so if you need anything, let me know. I'll have some pizza brought in and there will be plenty to drink in the kitchen. If there's anything else I can do for you at any point, just yell."

Jeff stayed at the front of the room as everyone stood and filed out. I was last in line and, just as I was about to walk out the door, Jeff stopped me.

"Can we talk for a second?" he asked quietly.

I sighed, turned around, and took the nearest seat.

Jeff closed the door and walked around the table to sit across from me, and I could tell he was nervous. I knew what was coming.

"I just wanted to talk about the other night, after dinner," he began.

"Is that so?" I asked. There was no way I was

going to make this easy on him.

"So, uh, Amy told me that you overheard us."

I nodded.

He clasped his hands together on the table and stared down at them. "Look, I know what's happened is entirely unprofessional on our part. I get that. But..." He paused, taking a deep breath and letting it out. "I just want to say that Amy means a lot to me. I certainly don't want to get her into any trouble. I know it's against policy to date a subordinate, but..." He trailed off and was silent for a moment before looking up at me. "Do you think you could maybe keep this quiet until we can figure out what to do?"

He looked so uncomfortable, like he might actually be in physical pain. Any other day, I would have reveled in the moment but, thanks to my own set of problems, I wasn't getting near as much joy out of it as I should have. Life was so unfair sometimes.

"You realize that you are basically asking me to lie for you?"

He nodded and looked back down at his hands. "I know. Believe me, this isn't easy. And I certainly wouldn't blame you if you walked out of here right now and went straight to HR to report me. If I were in your shoes, I would be appalled that my boss would ask me to do something like this."

For a brief moment, I almost felt sorry for the guy.

"If you do report us," he continued, "please don't mention Amy. I'll resign and walk out, no problem. I just don't want to ruin her career here." He looked back up at me and our eyes locked. "I'm begging you," he added. "Man to man. Please leave her out of it."

He really was taking all of the fun out of what

should have been the best day of my life. Maybe it was the look in his eyes or maybe it was the mess I had made with Sara that was throwing me off my game, but I felt a tiny piece of compassion inside.

"We'll see how it goes," I said, standing up and walking out. It was, after all, a very tiny piece.

Instead of going back to the tech room, I walked down to the cafeteria and bought two Twix bars. It was 3:30 and I was already behind schedule, thanks to Jeff.

When I reached the bench by the Virgin Mary, it was empty. I took a seat and stared at the statue for a while. Before my break was over, I stood and headed back inside, shoving both Twix bars into my pocket.

When I entered the tech room, I glanced over at Amy. She was looking at me, worry etched on her face. I continued on undeterred to my desk, where I tended to the tasks at hand, getting ready for 5:20.

At 5:00, Chip's giant head appeared above me.

"Well," he said, "this may be it. My last full day here."

I groaned. "You're not going to get laid off, Chip. Especially not on Monday."

"We'll see. Hey, good luck tonight. I hope everything goes well."

"Thanks," I said. Chip really was a pretty good guy. I hoped he could get through the weekend without worrying himself silly.

He sank out of sight, and I leaned back in my chair to relax for the next twenty minutes but was interrupted only moments later when he popped back up.

"I just got another hit," he whispered. "I'll send it to you." He sank out of sight, and I waited on his message.

As soon as I had the MAC address, I opened a command prompt and ran the getmac command against Dr. Carver's PC. It returned a match. I checked the RMM and confirmed it was his account that was currently logged in.

Chip reappeared. "I would love to stick around to see if you find anything, but I'm meeting my parents for dinner. Do you mind if I take off?"

"Not at all. Enjoy."

"See you Monday," he said and disappeared.

I leaned back, staring at my monitor, and thought. If the password change had kept any unauthorized users out, that meant it had to be Dr. Carver that was using the PC at that very moment. If only there was some way I could confirm that.

A simple idea struck me. I picked up the phone and looked up Dr. Carver's extension. If he answered, I would have him red-handed. As I was about to dial, another thought occurred to me. I didn't want to spook him with a call from IT if he was in the middle of something. Instead, I dialed Carrie's extension. Since it was a few minutes past 5:00, I wasn't actually expecting her to pick up, so I was pleasantly surprised when she did.

"Hey, Carrie," I said. "This is Eric from IT. We spoke the other day."

"Yes, I remember. How are you?" she asked.

"I'm good. I'm sure you got the memo that we are doing some migrations tonight and to make sure to close out of all applications but keep your PCs running, right?"

"Sure did," she said.

"Great. It will still be a few minutes before we

start, but I'm just calling with a friendly reminder and to see if anyone over there is still working."

"We've already logged out of everything over here. In fact, I had already left but I had to come back for my sunglasses. Otherwise, you wouldn't have caught me. I'll double-check with Dr. Carver on my way back out. He's still in his office, but he should be out of everything."

"Oh, no," I said, almost too enthusiastically. "That won't be necessary. I'll give him a ring. You go ahead and enjoy your weekend."

"Thank you, I'll do that."

I hung up and smiled.

Got you, you asshole.

A few moments later, I heard Jeff yell from the front of the room. "It's officially 5:20, guys. Proceed when ready."

I really wanted to see what Dr. Carver was up to, but I also needed to get started on the migration. Others would be waiting on me, and I didn't want to be the holdup. I contemplated the unsophisticated approach of just taking over his screen via our RMM software to see what was going on, but there was no guarantee there would be anything obvious happening. Plus, I didn't want to alert him that I was on to him and give him a chance to cover his tracks while I was occupied with my other, more pressing tasks.

Uttering a small curse, I switched focus to the migration. I started the refresh script before jumping into the existing SQL server to take the database offline and started the backup.

By the time I was done, the refresh scripts had finished, since not much data had changed from when I last ran it a 4 o'clock.

I started the tedious task of disabling the old shares and enabling the new ones. Somewhere in that process, the database backup completed, so I moved it to the new server and began the restore process before continuing with the shares. Once those were complete, I took a moment to think about Dr. Carver while the database restore continued to run.

If Dr. Carver was using a proxy to bypass the content filters, it simply meant that he was looking at or downloading something that he should not be looking at or downloading. If he was actually downloading something, maybe I could find what it was by taking a peek at his files.

I opened the file explorer on my PC and typed WS003-04-2c$ into the address bar. Because I was a network admin, the C drive on his computer opened right up for me. This allowed me to browse through the files on his computer without him seeing any evidence that I was doing so.

I started with the obvious places; his 'My Documents' folder and 'My Pictures' folder. If he was downloading something, it would likely be in one of those two places. I browsed through what few files he had but saw nothing out of the ordinary. I expanded my search but came up empty.

As I was contemplating my next move, I noticed the restore of the database had reached its completion. I once again switched focus and ran the first of the scripts Wyatt had given me. Since that one was supposed to take an hour to run, I decided to put aside Dr. Carver for the time being and start decommissioning the old domain controller.

****

Somewhere around 8:30 p.m., I stood up and stretched. Everyone had made their way into our small kitchen to have some of the pizza that had been delivered only a few minutes prior. It was good timing because I was finished with the domain controller and my stomach was growling for food.

I strolled into the kitchen and grabbed a paper plate and a slice of pepperoni. Jerry and Thomas were the only ones not present. They were likely in their offices, which were located down the hall from the tech room, doing whatever developers do.

"How's it going?" Jeff asked, focusing on his pizza.

"As planned," I mumbled with my mouth full. I took a moment to savor the deliciousness before swallowing. "The scripts are done. I'm about to do the checks that Wyatt gave me. If everything is good, then we're past the biggest hurdle."

I expected a hearty round of congratulations from everyone, but they all seemed more taken by the pizza than by my accomplishments. It was good pizza, though, so I couldn't blame them.

After several more pieces, I went back to my desk and ran the checks on HERK. Thankfully, everything came out as it should. I yelled across the room to Paul that he could start his tasks, then called Jerry to let him know HERK was all set. We wouldn't need to roll anything back at this point. All systems were go, at least as far as I was concerned. With the database out of the way, I could focus on my remaining items. It was looking more and more like I would be home well before daylight.

****

By 12:45 a.m., I had everything in place, with the exception of pushing out the new connection strings for HERK to all of the workstations on the network. I had yet to hear from Jerry on their testing, which was slightly worrisome. They should have been done well before then.

I picked up the phone to dial Jerry's extension but thought better of it. My back was getting stiff and my butt was going numb, so I thought a walk down to his office would do me some good.

Since Paul had already left for the night and the helpdesk duo of Jimmy and Pat were nowhere to be seen, the tech room was unusually quiet. I noticed the light in Jeff's office was on and his door was slightly cracked open, so I assumed he was in there napping.

When I reached the developer offices, Jerry's door was open. I walked in to find him at his desk with Thomas looking over his shoulder.

"I don't get it," he was saying.

"Don't get what?" I asked.

They both looked over at me. "We're having a problem getting the APIs to work on the new system. Our apps aren't connecting to HERK."

That didn't sound good.

"Maybe the changes Wyatt gave us are wrong," suggested Thomas.

"I don't think so," Jerry dismissed the idea. "We were getting returns from the test functions yesterday. Nothing would have changed between now and then."

"If that's the case, why are we getting a null set?" asked Thomas.

Jerry shook his head and leaned back in his chair.

"I wish I knew."

As much as I wanted to stand there and listen to other people's problems, I interjected. "So, can I go ahead and push out the new connection strings for HERK?"

Jerry shook his head. "I wouldn't if I were you."

"Why not?" I asked. "HERK is fine, right? It's just your add-ons that are the issue?"

"As best as we can tell, yes. But if we can't figure this out in the next few hours, we're going to have to roll everything back to the old system where it was working." Jerry explained.

"Wait a minute," I said, panic building. "Paul has already taken the old array offline and gone home."

"Then someone better get in touch with him and let him know he may be coming back."

"Shit," I muttered. "I'll let Jeff know."

I left Jerry's office with a sense of dread as my hopes of leaving before sunrise began to dwindle.

I walked back to the tech room to tell Jeff the bad news. As I approached his office, the door was still slightly ajar. I started to knock but stopped when I heard his voice.

"I don't know what more I can do?" he was saying. "I mean, we both gave it a shot, and we both got the same answer. I don't think we should push it anymore."

There was a pause before he spoke again.

"I know, I know," he said. "Believe me, if there was any way I could convince him I would."

Another pause.

"I know," he said again, much quieter so that I had to strain to hear. "I don't want to lose you either. We'll figure something out. I'll call you back when we're done here. Good night."

I waited a few seconds before knocking.

"Come in," he called out.

I pushed the door open to see Jeff sitting behind his desk, slumped in his chair. He looked tired, but he sat up straight when he saw me.

"The guys are having trouble getting their stuff connected to HERK on the new system," I told him. "They think there's a chance we might have to roll back."

He closed his eyes and pinched the bridge of his nose. "Great. I'll see if I can get in touch with Paul and make sure he keeps his phone on."

I left his office and went back to my desk. I opened the top drawer, where I had deposited the two Twix bars I had purchased earlier. I pulled one out, opened it, and took a bite.

As I sat there thinking about Jeff's conversation, I picked up my phone and looked at it. I still had not listened to the three voicemails that Sara had left when I skipped out on our dinner. Against my better judgment, I pulled up the first one.

Hey, where are you? I guess you're running late. Give me a call when you get this.

I hit seven to delete and listened as the second message played.

Hey, me again. I'm getting a little worried. Where are you? Call me.

I once again hit seven and listened to the last message. It started off with silence, and I was beginning to think it would be a hang-up until Sara spoke.

Me again. I assume dinner is off.

I could hear the disappointment dripping from her

voice.

Come on, Eric. Please don't flake out on me, not tonight.

There was another pause.

Sorry. I hope you're okay. I'll feel horrible if something bad happened.

The message ended, and I just sat there, staring at my desk. I eventually found the presence of mind to hang up the phone and place the partially eaten Twix bar back in the drawer.

It was just past 1 a.m. and I wanted nothing more than to talk to Sara.

****

A little after 1:30, Jimmy and Pat came back into the tech room, jarring me from my funk. I heard them report to Jeff that Jerry and Thomas were still working on the problem, then they went into the kitchen to presumably hog up all the leftover pizza.

I was in a holding pattern until further notice, so I decided to jump back into the Dr. Carver matter to take my mind off things.

I did a quick check on the MAC of his PC and wasn't surprised to see that it was back to its default address. I was sure he had finished whatever he was doing long ago, changed it back, and gone home.

I opened a remote session into the PC, and it came up at the login screen. I didn't know his password, of course, but that was just a formality. Being a network admin, I logged into the domain controller, found his user account in Active Directory, and reset it. I flipped back over to his PC and logged in with the new password of 'iamajerk123'.

I spent the next few minutes looking through his

browser history but found nothing. I did another check of his files just to make sure I didn't miss something earlier and to see if anything new had shown up, but nothing had. I checked to see if a proxy address was defined in the connection settings of the browser but again came up empty.

I contemplated giving up and checking the kitchen for any remaining pizza, but I could overhear Jimmy and Pat's inane conversation about video games and didn't want to risk getting pulled into it. Instead, I kept clicking. I checked the Recycle Bin, but it was empty. I checked the cache and recent files, but there was nothing there. I was about to move on when I paused, realizing that was unusual. There was always something there, unless someone went out of their way to remove it.

What have you been up to?

Dr. Asshat was obviously hiding something. Normal users didn't clean their temp and recent files if they weren't. Luckily for me, deleted files could easily be recovered using one of many available undelete utilities, even if the recycle bin had been emptied. Most people didn't know that when you delete a file, the Operating System simply marks the space where the file was stored as being available for new data to be written there. The original data stays put until something else comes along and overwrites that space. And, unless you are constantly creating new files, the chances of that space being used immediately is slim, leaving old data to linger.

I quickly downloaded one of the utilities and started it. It would take a few minutes to scan the drive, so I sat back and waited. Roughly ten minutes later, a list of files popped up that could potentially be recovered. I was going to focus on the temp folder first, but I noticed a long list of image files with numbers for names.

Well, well, well. What have we here?

I had a good idea what I was looking at from experience. A person didn't have to be in IT too long before running across someone's stash of adult photos.

I looked back to make sure the wonder twins were still in the kitchen. The last thing I wanted was one of them walking by while I was confirming what I suspected. They were still engrossed in their video game conversation and eating pizza. I peeked around the front corner of my cube to make sure Jeff was still in his office. His door was closed, and he was nowhere in sight, so I assumed I was safe.

I clicked on one of the image files and hit the preview button. The second it opened, I frantically started clicking to close it. When it was gone, I sat back in my chair in disbelief. I had been half right.

****

I spent the next hour staring at my monitor where the image had been and waiting for word from Jerry and Thomas. My mind was racing as I tried to figure out what to do. I knew I should immediately report what I had found. It was, after all, far beyond the normal adult content. It was FBI territory. Prison territory. I stood up and took a step away from my desk, but paused and sat back down.

It was just after 2:30 a.m. and we were only thirty minutes away from the drop-dead time, but that didn't matter much to me at that moment. Rolling back would suck, but I would only play a small part in it, even though it meant staying longer. If Jerry and Thomas figured out the issue in the next thirty minutes, I would have more work to do, but it would take much less time to do it.

My bigger concern was that I had less than thirty minutes to figure out what I was going to do about what I had found. I knew I simply needed to wash my hands of it by reporting it to Jeff and moving aside. I wrestled with it for several minutes before standing up to go to Jeff's office. As I turned to leave my cubicle, my eye happened across my phone and I stopped.

I could hear Sara's last message in my head.

Slowly, I sat back down, staring at the phone. A thought was forming in my mind. I let it coalesce until the time on my workstation said 2:50, at which point I sprang into action.

I checked to make sure Jimmy and Pat were still engaged in their stupid conversation, then checked for Jeff.

I pulled Word up and began banging out text. When I was finished, I quickly read through my work. It only lacked one final touch.

I checked again to make sure the coast was clear. With Jimmy and Pat being in the kitchen, I would only have a few seconds notice if they decided to get up and walk out into the tech room. I cursed my cubicle location as I tried to position myself in front of my monitor enough to block it from view, just in case. I pulled up the remote session into Dr. Carver's PC, hit preview on the image file once again, and grabbed a screen capture. My hands were shaking, and I kept glancing back toward the kitchen to keep an eye out for movement. Having what I needed, I closed the undelete utility on Dr. Carver's PC, logged out and exited the session.

I quickly added the image I had captured to the Word document and paused. I knew I couldn't send the file via email because I wanted as little of an electronic trail as I could possibly make. I needed to print it.

The only problem was that the printer was at the front of the room, close to Jeff's office.

I took a deep breath and checked again to make sure no one was moving and hit print. I closed the file without saving it and stood up, walking briskly to the printer.

I was still ten feet away when Jeff's office door swung open and he came out. The printer was halfway between us and had already started spitting out the document. I thoroughly panicked on the inside while trying to remain calm on the outside. It was all I could do to not sprint the remaining distance. If Jeff saw what I had just printed, I would have some serious explaining to do. I needed to reach the printer before him without being obvious about it. I needed a miracle.

And then Thomas appeared in the doorway.

"It's done," he yelled. "We got it working."

Jeff stopped to look over at him as I kept walking.

"Thank God." Jeff breathed a deep sigh of relief and turned back to his office. "I'll let Paul know he can go to bed."

"It's all yours," Thomas said to me before turning and disappearing.

I grabbed the sheet of paper from the printer, my hands shaking, folded it in half, and took it back to my desk. I fished an envelope from my bottom desk drawer and had just stuffed the letter in when Jimmy's voice, immediately behind me, made me jump.

"Are we rolling back?" he had asked.

"Jesus," I said. "Don't sneak up on me like that."

He laughed and said he was sorry, but I didn't believe him for one minute. If I would have had my way, everyone in the IT department would have been wearing cowbells.

"They got it fixed. We're moving forward as planned," I explained.

"Awesome," he said.

I nonchalantly slid the envelope into my desk drawer next to the opened Twix bar. "I'll start pushing out the connection strings," I told him just as Pat arrived and stood next to him. "I'll let you guys know if there are any failures so you can run them down."

"Cool," said Pat, "maybe we'll actually have something to do now."

They high-fived each other, and I shook my head and sighed. "I would rather you not stand over my shoulder while I do this. I need to concentrate. I'll let you know if I need you."

"Yes sir." They both saluted and headed back into the kitchen.

"Christ," I muttered and got to work.

While I was waiting for the scripts to run and the results to be returned, I pulled the envelope out of the drawer, sealed it, and wrote 'Dr. Carver' on the outside. I folded it over twice and shoved it into my pocket.

When the scripts finished, I checked the output. There were fourteen PCs that had failed. All in all, that wasn't too bad. Most, if not all of those, were likely just powered off. Honestly, I had expected more users to ignore the memo directing them to leave their PCs on for the night. I know I myself rarely read any of the memos I received.

I sent two copies of the failure list to the printer, then yelled, "Hey, nerds."

I heard chairs scraping on the floor in the kitchen. Seconds later, Jimmy and Pat appeared outside my cubicle.

"There were fourteen failures," I said. "There are two copies of the list in the printer." I pulled two thumb drives out of my top desk drawer that I had prepared earlier in the week. Each contained the connection strings. I handed one to each of them. "The scripts are on these. Just run them manually on each machine. Make sure HERK opens before you move on."

"Aye, aye, Captain," said Jimmy. They both saluted again before heading off.

I turned back to my monitor and began the last few cleanup tasks I needed to do. I knew it would be a while before Jimmy and Pat reported back, since the PCs in question were spread throughout the entire hospital.

****

At 4:45, the dynamic duo returned and reported that all the failed PCs were taken care of. It had taken them a little longer than I thought it would, but it was done. I thanked them for their help and asked them to wait in the kitchen while I got Jeff for a quick wrap-up meeting, so he could sign off on the night's labors.

I knocked on his office door and heard him faintly say to come in. When I opened the door, he looked like he had run a marathon.

"We're done," I announced. "We'll be in the kitchen when you're ready."

"Thanks. I'll be right there."

"By the way, you look like hell," I observed. "You okay?"

One corner of his mouth turned up in a small grin. "Yeah," he said. "It's just been a long night."

I had no idea what he had been doing there, tucked away in his office for the entire night, other than the phone call to Amy I had overheard. It certainly wasn't *actual* work, but whatever it was seemed to have taken a toll on him. Maybe he just wasn't used to being up past his bedtime.

I walked back to the kitchen and noticed there was one slice of pizza left among the pile of boxes on the table.

"Thanks for leaving some for the rest of us," I said.

"No problem," Pat said, obviously missing my sarcasm.

I put the slice on a paper plate and grabbed a bottle of water from the counter by the sink. It was room temperature, but it would do.

As I sat down, Jeff walked in and leaned against the counter with a notepad in his hand.

"All right. Let's go through the list," he directed.

He began reading through his checklist and I replied to each item in turn. When he got to the end and asked about the connection strings, Jimmy and Pat answered that they had finished the list I gave them.

"Perfect," said Jeff. He looked at me. "All the rest of them were successful?"

"Actually, I found one more just a few minutes ago. It's no big deal. I'll take care of it on the way out."

"Fine by me," he agreed, scribbling on the notepad. "That looks like it. You guys are free to go."

"Sweet," said Jimmy and Pat in unison. I fought

the urge to choke them both as they got up and left.

Jeff walked over and plopped down at the table. He really did look like hell.

I slid my plate in his direction. "Here, why don't you have this," I offered.

"Thanks, but I'm not really hungry."

My thoughts immediately jumped to the overheard phone conversation between him and Amy, then to Sara's voicemail.

"Yeah, me neither."

I stood up, leaving the plate where it was. "Let's get out of here."

"You go ahead. I'll get the lights."

For some reason, sitting there slumped in a chair in our crappy little kitchen, he looked completely defeated and broken. For the first time ever, I truly did feel sorry for him.

"Suit yourself," I said and walked out.

****

Instead of going straight to the parking lot, I made my way over to the labs through the mostly empty hallways, passing only the occasional night shift nurse or late-night visitor. There was no last-minute find to take care of as I had told Jeff, I simply needed an excuse to stay behind.

When I reached the labs, the area was deserted and most of the lights were off. I made my way quietly to Dr. Carver's office door. It was shut and probably locked, but that didn't matter.

I paused and thought of Sara and what she had said to me two days ago in the cafeteria.

Dr. Carver could just make my life miserable until I can't take it anymore and quit.

And what she had said the previous evening, a day after I had screwed everything up.

I got suspended indefinitely, pending a review next week. I'm certain Dr. Carver is going to fire me.

I pulled the envelope from my pocket, flattened it out, knelt, and slid it under the door.

"Take that, asshole," I muttered to myself as I left.

****

As I exited the building, the sky was a deep blue with the first signs of daylight. A few cars passed by out on Rogers Avenue, but for the most part, it was still and quiet and the cool air felt fantastic. I walked slowly to my Explorer, starting to feel the long night catch up to me. As I walked between a row of cars, I glanced to my left and happened to see Jeff and Amy standing next to his truck, facing each other. They reached out and held each other's hands as they talked.

I paused for a moment, watching them from around the corner of an SUV. I couldn't tell for sure from that distance, but neither of them looked to be happy.

I started to move on but stopped. "Shit," I mumbled and walked toward them.

As I approached, Amy noticed me first and stopped talking. Jeff followed her gaze and slowly dropped her hands from his when he saw me.

Neither of them spoke as I reached them and stopped. I looked around for a moment, uncomfortable and unsure of how to proceed. Finally, I found what I wanted to say.

"So, you two are serious?" I asked.

They looked at each other and both nodded. I looked down at my feet, then over at the hospital, then out to Rogers Avenue and finally back to them.

"I haven't told anyone," I said. "And I'm not going to."

They looked from me to each other and back to me. I thought I saw a gleam in both of their eyes.

A hint of a smile touched Amy's lips and she started to speak but I held up a hand to stop her.

"I wish both of you the best. Don't let this place or me or anything else get in your way."

As I walked off, I wondered what the hell was happening to me. Not only had I felt sorry for Jeff only minutes earlier, I was also missing a golden opportunity to use the dirt I had on him and Amy to make his life miserable. I shook my head in disgust and pretended it was lack of sleep.

Chapter 11

Saturday, May 25th, 2002

Ten minutes after I left Jeff and Amy in the
parking lot of St. Edwards, I turned into the lot at my
apartment and began to realize the physical and
emotional toll the previous day and night had taken on
me. I was exhausted. I managed to park and climb out
of my vehicle. My shoes felt like lead weights as I
crossed the lot to my apartment. As I unlocked my
door, I glanced in the direction of Sara's building. I
knew better than to attempt to talk to her in the state I
was in. And besides, her building looked so far away at
that moment.

I entered my apartment, locked the door behind
me, went straight to the couch, and fell flat on my face.

****

I didn't sleep well as the day wore on. I awoke
often and tossed and turned. I got up several times to
use the restroom, to eat, to take my shoes off, but I
always returned to the couch for another round of fitful
sleep. At some point, I had turned on the TV and muted
the volume. It was still on at 7:00 that evening when I
woke up for the last time. Even though it had been over
twelve hours since I had first hit the couch, I felt only
slightly rested.

I knew I couldn't sit around the apartment much

longer without going crazy, so I put on my shoes and grabbed my keys from the coffee table.

When I hopped into my Explorer, I wasn't exactly sure where I was going, I just felt the need to go.

As I drove, I thought about everything that had happened the past few days. I thought about the previous night, and I thought about what the coming days might hold. As I thought, I realized there was one person I needed to go see.

On the way across town, I made one quick stop to pick up a pizza before pulling into an apartment complex that I had only been to once before. I found apartment 12 and knocked on the door.

When Chip answered, he looked confused.

"Hey, Eric," he greeted me. "What are you doing here?"

"Mind if I come in?" I asked, holding up the pizza. "I brought food."

"Not at all." He stepped aside. "What's this about? Did something go wrong with the migration?"

"No," I told him as I sat the pizza on his coffee table. "The migration went pretty well."

"That's good," he said, looking confused again. "So, then, why are you here?" He asked it in the nicest, most likable way that only he could.

I shrugged. "No reason. I just felt like a pizza, and I thought you might want some, too."

"You know me," he said, patting his oversized stomach. "I never say no to food. I'll grab some plates. You want a soda?"

"Sure." I took a seat in a chair that sat at an angle next to the couch, where his open laptop lay. "I hope I'm not interrupting anything."

"I was just looking through some more job boards," he said, returning with two plates and a roll of paper towels.

"Finding anything?" I asked.

"Nope."

He returned to the kitchen and came back with two cans of Dr. Pepper. He shoved his laptop aside and sat down on the couch as I opened the pizza box, and we both dug in.

"So, did you have time to look into that latest hit on the proxy?" he asked.

I took a large bite of pizza and shook my head. "Nope," I lied around the mouthful of food. "But I've got a few good ideas I'll try next week. Hey, do you watch Star Trek Enterprise?"

"Uh, yeah," he answered, perking up. "Of course, I do. Do you?"

I nodded. "What kind of person wouldn't?"

We spent the next few hours finishing off the pizza and talking about an array of things that had nothing to do with work. It was nice getting to know a little more about Chip. He was the closest thing I had to a friend among my immediate coworkers, and I was ashamed I didn't know more than I did. I asked a lot of questions, and he seemed to thoroughly enjoy answering them.

When the clock struck 10:00 p.m., I was once again feeling the effects of the last twenty-four hours. I stood up to leave, and Chip followed me out into the cool night air.

"Thanks for stopping by," he said. "I had fun."

"Me too." I opened my car door and slid into the seat. It felt good to have taken Chip's mind off job searches and layoffs, if only for a few hours. "See you

Monday."

"See you Monday," he repeated.

I closed the door, started the engine, and headed to my apartment.

****

When I pulled into an empty spot and switched off the engine, I didn't climb out right away because I was just too tired. I looked at the last building to the left and wondered if Sara was still awake. It was late, but not that late.

After a few more moments, I pushed the door open and climbed out, shutting and locking it behind me. I walked slowly to my apartment, not really looking forward to being alone. I stopped to look once again in the direction of Sara's apartment, but I just couldn't gather the courage to go knock on her door.

As I entered my apartment, I flipped on the light switch and stood in the doorway, looking at the pathetic little room. Sure, I had overspent on the TV, the couch, and the coffee table, but from where I was standing, it all looked worthless. I sighed and closed the door, making sure it was locked, and plopped down on the couch. I dug my phone out of my pocket and held it in my hand, looking at the darkened screen. I wanted to text Sara, or call, or something. Instead, I sat it on the coffee table next to the remote.

I kicked off my shoes and was about to lay over on the couch when the phone lit up and vibrated. The caller ID showed Sara's number. I picked it and hit the answer button.

"Hey," I said.

There was no immediate reply, and I thought for a moment she had accidentally pocket dialed me.

"Hey," she finally spoke.

I searched for something to say, for the right words, but as usual, I couldn't find them. I settled on the only thing I could think of.

"How are you?" I asked.

There was a pause, and I heard something like a sharp intake of breath. When Sara spoke, it sounded like she was starting to cry.

"I just have a few things that I need to say to you," she said. "I want you to understand that you really hurt me."

I sat up straight on the couch. "Sara, I'm so, so sorry—"

"No," she interrupted. "You don't get to apologize. Not this time. Just be quiet and listen."

I kept quiet but started sliding my shoes back on.

"I just can't believe, that after all this time, I mean nothing to you."

I wanted to interrupt, to tell her that wasn't true. Sure, I was an idiot and was often clueless, but that just wasn't true. I knew that if I said something, though, she would hang up. I owed it to her to do as she said, to just shut up and listen.

"Did you ever wonder why I've barely dated since college? Especially since you moved back here?"

I wasn't sure if I was supposed to answer, so I took the cautious approach and stayed quiet.

"God," she continued. "I can't believe I was so stupid to ever think that…"

She paused and it sounded like she was blowing her nose. I finished putting on my shoes and stood up.

"I cared about you, Eric. A lot," she said softly, almost inaudible. I could hear the tears in her voice.

I hit the mute button on my phone as I crossed my tiny living room and opened the front door.

"But I guess you don't think about me the way I've always thought about you." She took in a sharp breath as I closed my door behind me, turned right, and started jogging up the sidewalk.

"When I think about that," she continued. "I wish I never knew you."

I felt like I had been physically punched and I almost tripped over my own feet. I caught myself and kept going.

"I'm sorry to bother you with this, but I just needed to get it off my chest."

I slid to a stop outside her door and paused to catch my breath before knocking.

"We can't be friends anymore," she continued, her voice breaking.

Her words rocked me back on my heels, but I steadied myself and knocked again.

"I have to go. Please don't contact me anymore," she finished and hung up.

I waited, still catching my breath, for what felt like hours, but was only a few moments until the door cracked open. There was a pause as I'm sure she contemplated slamming it in my face, but she pulled it farther open and stood there, looking at me. I could see the tears on her cheeks.

"You're wrong," I told her. "If you think I don't care about you, you're wrong. I know I'm oblivious, and I know I haven't given you any reason to think otherwise, but I promise you, you're wrong. I see that now. And if you'll just give me a second chance, I swear I will prove it to you."

She shut the door and locked it.

Chapter 12

Sunday May 26th, 2002

I awoke the next morning as the first light of day began to seep through the blinds in my living room. I had spent the night on the couch, alternating between small bouts of restless sleep and much larger bouts of insomnia and feeling like the worst person in the world. I had spent a lot of time thinking about what Sara had said, about how she thought of me. And mostly, I thought about how I had never paid attention.

I stood up and stretched, aching all over, and walked to the window. Peeking out between two slats, I could see Sara's Camry was still in the parking lot. I was about to turn away, when I caught sight of her walking toward her car, carrying her pink duffel bag.

I wanted to run out and stop her, to try once again to explain myself, but I didn't. I turned away and headed to the bathroom, glancing at the clock as I went. It was 6:45.

I got undressed and hopped in the shower, where I spent the next thirty minutes completely exhausting the hot water supply.

After drying off and putting on clean clothes, I felt much less refreshed than I had hoped I would. I decided some food might help, so I went to the kitchen and fixed a plate of scrambled eggs with three slices of bacon.

I sat down on the couch to eat. The food was fine, but it just didn't taste as good as it usually did.

First my Twix, now this, I thought, but I kept eating until everything was gone.

After putting my plate in the sink, I sat back down on the couch and wondered what I was going to do with myself for the remainder of the day. It was only 7:45. I had a long, long way to go, so I stared at the walls, willing the time to pass, until I drifted off to sleep.

When I woke up, I checked the time. It was just after 8:30. I had only been asleep for half an hour, at best.

Wishing I could sleep the entire day away, but knowing it wasn't going to happen, I turned on the TV, which was tuned to channel 5, the local CBS affiliate. I was about to start flipping through the channels when the local news anchor appeared.

"Good morning everyone," he said. "We have some breaking news this morning. A bridge over the Arkansas River has collapsed near the town of Webbers Falls, Oklahoma. Authorities say the bridge, which is on Interstate 40, collapsed when it was hit by a barge about 7:50 this morning. Details are sketchy at this moment, but there are believed to be multiple fatalities."

I stopped breathing as I pictured Sara walking across the parking lot with her pink duffel bag, the one she always took when going to her parent's house. It had been 6:45 when I turned from the window and headed to the shower. It was about an hour drive to Webbers Falls without making any stops along the way. That would have put her there about 7:45. Of course, if she had stopped for gas or food, that would have put her four or five minutes behind.

I broke out of my trance, grabbed my phone, and frantically hit buttons until I managed to call Sara's number. I got a message back saying all circuits were busy. I took the phone away from my ear and looked at it, dumbfounded, then hung up and redialed, getting the same result.

"Shit," I said aloud. "Shit, shit, shit." I stood up and paced the floor. On the TV, they were showing distant, aerial footage of the bridge. I froze when I saw it. My heart was pounding in my ears and I could no longer hear the sounds coming from the TV.

I dialed again. "Come on, come on," I groaned as I waited. When I got the same message, I almost threw the phone across the room.

I tried to compose myself. Surely Sara was fine. What were the chances that she would be crossing the bridge at that exact moment? Surely they were astronomical.

I sat down on the couch and stared at the TV, not really seeing anything, until I eventually picked up the remote and turned it off.

I dialed again, expecting the same message. When I heard a ring on the other end, I jumped up from the couch feeling excited and anxious. I started pacing back and forth.

"Come on, answer," I said. As the phone continued to ring, I slowly started to lose my excitement. I kept pacing and the phone kept ringing. "Come on," I yelled. I let it keep ringing until it eventually stopped. No answer. Not even voicemail picked up.

At a loss, I did the only thing I could think to do. I

grabbed my wallet and keys and ran out the door with all kinds of terrible images bouncing around in my head.

****

Rather than take our usual route through Fort Smith and into Oklahoma, I jumped onto I-540 and headed north. It was a much less direct route, but it allowed me to bypass most of town and it meant I could travel at a higher rate of speed.

I pushed my old Explorer as fast as I dared, hoping there were no state troopers around. Between Fort Smith and Van Buren, 540 crossed the Arkansas River as it snaked its way east toward the Mississippi. As I hit the bridge, I glanced out at the waters below before snapping back to the road as panic welled inside me. I forced myself to focus on the task at hand and not think of anything else.

Not far past the river, I-540 joined I-40. Once I was on and heading west, I again pushed the Explorer as hard as I dared and hoped there were no police set up anywhere along the way.

Thankfully, being a Sunday morning, traffic was light and there was little to slow me up. As I drove, I tried calling several more times, but each time the phone just rang until it went silent. Eventually, I quit trying and just focused on getting there as fast as I could.

Despite making record time, the drive felt like an eternity and the closer I got, the more nervous I became. Several miles out, traffic increased and slowed down. Less than a mile from the river, cars were being diverted onto exit 291, to the small town of Gore, where Highway 64 crossed the river into Webbers Falls.

As I exited and turned right onto Highway 10, I wanted to scream. Being only a two-lane road, I was at the mercy of the line of traffic ahead of me. There was also plenty of oncoming traffic being routed from the other side of the river, so there were no opportunities to pass. Even if there were, it would have done no good. The line in front of me stretched out of sight.

Several miles later, Highway 10 ran into Highway 64, which was also only two lanes. I turned left, following the line of cars.

As we neared Gore, traffic slowed considerably, and I grew more and more frustrated and frantic. Up ahead, I could see the stop sign where 64 joined with Main Street. It seemed to be taking forever for each car to make the left turn. I contemplated pulling onto the narrow shoulder and hitting the gas but talked myself out of it.

Finally, my turn came. I hardly stopped at the stop sign, staying close to the car in front of me as they turned. I rode their bumper the few hundred feet to the bridge. As we crossed, I looked to my left downstream. The I-40 bridge was only visible from the west end of the Highway 64 bridge. As I crossed, I kept glancing to my left until it came into view. When I saw it, I was mesmerized. Close to the right-hand bank, a section of the bridge hung down at a steep angle, touching the water, like a trap door that had fallen open. I could see the barge at the base, as well as what looked like other, smaller boats in the water nearby. I forced myself not to think of what might be happening there at this moment.

When I looked back up at the road, the car in front of me had slowed almost to a stop. I slammed on my brakes, tires screeching, and braced for impact.

Miraculously, I was able to avoid a collision. The car behind me honked, but I paid it no attention. I could see my turn just up ahead.

When I reached North Stand Watie Boulevard, I needed to turn left, but the long line of slow oncoming traffic was blocking me. I put on my blinker, hoping someone would be kind enough to stop and let me through. After waiting as long I could stand, which wasn't long at all, I saw a small gap between a pickup and a semi. I tensed and waited until the right moment, and hit the gas, cutting the wheel and flying through the gap, narrowly missing the big rig's front bumper. I barely paid attention to its blaring horn as I sped away down Stand Watie until I came up on a slow-moving car in front of me. Commercial was only a block away, but rather than stay behind the car, I turned onto Hayes. One block up, I took a hard right turn onto Sixth, holding my breath and barely keeping control of both the Explorer and myself.

The Bartlett house was one block away and as I slid to a stop in front of it, half in the ditch, I saw Sara's Camry sitting in the driveway. I closed my eyes and leaned my head on the steering wheel and began breathing again. I had never been happier to see that car.

After a few moments, I shifted into park, killed the engine, and climbed out. As I walked up the drive and started opening the gate, I heard the screen door open. I looked up to see Sara standing on the porch.

"Eric?" she said. "What are you doing here?"

I stopped cold as I stared at her, transfixed. She was wearing faded blue jeans and a white t-shirt, and she had never looked more beautiful.

She started to speak again but stopped as I willed my feet to move and quickly covered the ground between us. I jumped up onto the porch, wrapped my arms around her, and held her as tight as I dared.

"Thank God you're okay," I whispered. "Thank God you're okay."

She slowly embraced me back and for the first time in as long as I could remember, tears began streaming down my face.

****

I didn't stay long that day. At some point, Sara's parents had joined us on the porch, each wrapping their arms around us. No one spoke. Eventually, Mr. and Mrs. Bartlett went back inside, and I let go of Sara.

There were so many things that I wanted to tell her, but I didn't. I knew I would probably screw it up anyway, so I stayed quiet as I walked to the Explorer. Sara followed me only as far as the gate. She never said a word, but as I started the engine and pulled away, she waved goodbye.

Joining the line of traffic snaking its way along Highway 64, I was content to drive slowly. I didn't look downstream as I crossed the river. Only when I was off the bridge did I realize I had been holding my breath.

As I drove, I thought about a lot of things. I thought about the sadness and horror of what was happening at that bridge. I thought about Amelia and Trevor and Amy and Jeff and Chip and life.

And I thought about Sara.

I wasn't sure how long we had been standing there on her parent's porch holding onto each other, but I realized those minutes would likely be the best of my life for a long time to come.

Chapter 13

Tuesday, May 28th, 2002
Two Days After

I waved at Marge as I walked into the cafeteria. Glancing to my right, in the direction of my usual table, I was surprised to see Sara sitting there. I took a twenty-dollar bill out of my pocket and tossed it on the counter.

"The usual, Marge," I said and walked away.

As I approached Sara, she looked up at me, and I thought I saw a trace of a smile, although it was likely wishful thinking.

"Hey. What are you doing here?"

She shrugged. "I really don't know for sure."

I stood there for a moment, not wanting to assume I could join her, but not wanting to walk away. She seemed to sense my predicament.

"You can sit down," she told me.

As I took a seat, I noticed the plastic containers in front of her, likely filled with all sorts of disgusting and healthy foods. I also noticed her ID badge clipped to her shirt collar.

She saw me looking at the items. "I started back to work today," she explained.

"That's great," I said, doing my best to contain my excitement.

"It was the strangest thing," she continued. "Dr.

Carver called me yesterday morning to tell me. He didn't say anything other than I can start back today."

I made a noncommittal noise, just to prove I was listening.

"And what's even more amazing, is that when I got here this morning, he handed me the paperwork recommending Amelia for the trial in Tulsa and asked me to submit it."

"That's awesome." I struggled much harder to keep a blank face. "Did he say why he changed his mind?"

"No, he just asked me to submit it and walked away."

"Well, how about that?"

"But that's not all," she continued. "I just heard he turned in his resignation, effective at the end of this week."

"Sounds like it's been quite a week in the lab." I stood up; I could no longer keep from smiling.

"Yeah," she agreed. "Why do you have that goofy grin on your face?"

"No reason," I lied as I tried to stop, but couldn't. "I'm just glad you're back."

"Thanks." She studied me, looking slightly suspicious.

There were still so many things I wanted to tell her, but once again I held myself in check. I was just happy that she was speaking to me at all.

"If you'll excuse me," I said, "I need to be getting back to work. I just remembered an extremely important matter I need to take care of."

I turned and walked away just as Marge was approaching with my tray of food.

"I won't be needing that after all, Marge, my dear,"

I said as I passed by her. "It's all yours."

****

Back at my desk, I was giddy with excitement and nerves. I couldn't believe my ridiculous plan actually seemed to be working. I knew that things between Sara and me were still very shaky and tentative, but at least it looked like one thing might be going my way.

I took a few deep breaths to calm myself and thought back to Friday night, during the migration. Although it had only been a few days, it felt likes weeks had passed, but I could still see the letter I had printed out and slid under Dr. Carver's office door plainly in my mind.

In it, I had stated that I knew what he was doing. I had even added the photo as proof, which had been a seriously risky move, but one that appeared as though it would pay off.

I went on to explain that I had been monitoring his activity for a while, and although that wasn't technically true, I figured a little white lie never hurt anyone.

I then got down to business, listing my demands. He was to lift Sara's suspension and recommend Amelia for the trial by the end of Wednesday. After that, he was to tender his resignation, effective at the end of the week. As long as I heard of those things happening, I would not go to the authorities with what I had found. Instead, the evidence would go away, and he could ride off into the sunset and never look back.

I didn't identify myself or give any contact method. He would simply have to assume the letter was serious and do what it asked, or risk suffering the consequences of his actions.

Not only did it work, but he came through a day early.

I sat there for a few minutes, thinking about what I was about to do.

I considered leaving well enough alone. After all, Sara had her job back, Amelia was being recommended for the trial, and Dr. Carver would no longer be there to make Sara's life miserable if he chose to do so. What more could I have asked for?

The image of the photo flashed in my mind, reinforcing my decision. I picked up the phone and dialed Carrie's extension.

"Hello, this is Carrie," she answered cheerfully.

"Hey, Carrie. It's Eric from IT again."

"Hey, Eric. How are you?"

"I'm great. Sorry to bother you, but I was wondering if Dr. Carver was in his office?"

"He stepped out for lunch about fifteen minutes ago. Do you want me to transfer you to his voicemail?"

"No thanks, I'll try back later," I said and hung up.

I opened a remote session into Dr. Carver's PC and re-ran the undelete utility, pulling up the list of deleted images.

I could hear Chip in his cubicle, eating his lunch at his desk.

"Hey, Chip?"

"Yeah?" he answered without poking his head over the wall.

"You're not going to believe what I just found. You should probably go get Jeff and come look at this."

Dr. Carver didn't know it at that moment, but the last line of my letter to him was also a little white lie.

****

I had given Jeff a very quick rundown of what Chip and I had been tracking the past few days and how I came to find what I was about to show them. I warned them that what they were going to see was disturbing, to say the least.

As soon as Jeff had seen one of the images, he had called the director, who showed up within minutes. Once he saw the image and heard the short rundown, he immediately called security to have them confiscate Dr. Carver's PC. His next call had been to the authorities. The next few hours were a bit of a blur.

Later that day, as I sat on the bench, eating my 3 o'clock Twix and thinking about how quickly things had unfolded, I couldn't help but feel relieved. Even though there was the high probability that Dr. Carver would turn over the letter I had written to the authorities, it didn't matter to me. So what if I had blackmailed him? He deserved it, and I would take whatever punishment came from that.

The kid sat next to me as usual, and we both watched several police cars come and go.

"I wonder what that's all about?" I asked with a grin.

The kid shrugged and kept munching on his Twix.

"Whatever it is," I said, "it sure looks like someone is in serious trouble."

When we were finished eating, I stood up and took his empty wrapper.

"Well, Trev, I don't know what the future holds for either one of us, but I just want you to know I have really enjoyed our talks."

He smiled and nodded, looking down at the gravel he was kicking.

"Tell your mom I said hello."

I turned and walked away, passing by the parked police cars on my way in. As I had told Trevor, I wasn't sure what the future held, but I was sure of one thing—my Twix had never tasted better.

Chapter 14

Friday, November 29th, 2002
Six Months After

I looked at the clock and saw that it was quitting time, so I wrapped up what I was working on and locked my workstation.

It had taken several months, but work had returned to some semblance of normalcy. The layoffs had come and gone. Chip had survived it, as had I, and I couldn't help but think that our discovery had played a major role in that.

Sara had survived it as well, no doubt based on her passion for the job and the fact that a doctor's salary had been temporarily freed up.

I had spent those first few months wondering when the authorities were going to show up at my door and ask why I hadn't turned Dr. Carver in right away and why I had blackmailed him, but the knock never came. Eventually I quit worrying, even though I knew it could still happen.

I put my coat on, grabbed my things, and stepped around to Chip's cubicle.

"Have a good weekend, Chip."

He looked up from his screen. "Is it 5 o'clock already?"

"Yep. Time flies when you're having fun."

"I guess so. See you later."

I walked to Jeff's office and found him on his cell phone.

"See you in a few," he said into the phone and hung up as I walked in through the open door.

"You ready?" I asked.

"Ready," he said, grabbing his keys from his desk drawer.

We walked out of the tech room, past the empty desk that used to belong to Amy.

As we made our way through the hallways, I kept glancing at his shoes until he eventually noticed.

"Why are you looking at my shoes?" he asked.

"I'm trying to figure out if they fit you," I said.

"Of course, they fit me. Why would I buy the wrong size shoes?"

"Not fit like that," I corrected him. "I mean, do they suit you?"

He gave me a sidelong glance. "Why are you trying to figure that out?"

"I have this pair of shoes that I love, but Sara says they don't fit me, and I have no idea why not. Now I just walk around all day looking at people's feet, wondering if the shoes they have on suit them or not, but I just can't tell. They all look fine to me."

"I see," he said. "And here I thought you were just being weird."

"Nope," I responded. "Not this time, anyway."

When we reached the lobby, Sara was waiting for us by the sliding glass doors.

"Hey," I said as we approached her. We hugged and I savored every single second of holding her in my arms.

For the past six months, since that moment on her parent's porch when I had realized that she was the most important and precious thing in my life, I had worked diligently to repair what I had broken. We were both tentative and unsure at first, especially Sara, but who could blame her? All I could hope for was that, over time, she would see I was no longer the self-centered jerk I used to be, and that I would never be that person again. As the months had passed, we had begun slowly bridging the gap between us. There was still work to do, but I was ecstatic to have the chance to do it.

"You ready for a fun-filled evening?" I asked, holding the hug as long as I could.

"Yes, but you are going to have to let me go or we'll be late," she said.

I smiled and let her go, wishing I could have held on just a little longer.

"Hey, Jeff, how are you?" she asked, turning her attention from me.

"Good. I like your shoes. They really fit you."

"Thanks." She glanced at me as though I should clearly see that they did. I made a mental note to punch Jeff in the face later.

We walked out into the chilly evening. The sun was already hanging low on the horizon as the days were getting shorter and shorter. As we crossed the lot, I could see Amy up ahead, leaning against Jeff's truck with her hands stuffed deep into her coat pockets and a scarf tied around her neck.

"Hey, guys," she greeted us as we approached.

"Hey, Amy," said Sara; the two of them hugged. "I love your scarf."

"Thank you. My mom bought it for me." She turned and gave me a hug. "Hey, Eric, how are you?"

"Well, my boss is a bit of a hard ass, but other than that, I'm good. How's Superior Federal?"

"It's going great," she said, laughing.

Along with two other IT guys, Amy had not made it through the layoffs. After three weeks of looking, she found and took a job in the IT department of Superior Federal Bank and genuinely seemed to love it. She worked in their offices just up the road from the hospital, across from the mall. I was very happy for her, mostly because getting laid off meant she and Jeff could continue dating without any worries and, although they made me want to puke sometimes, they really were good together.

Amy gave Jeff a quick kiss. "I'm starving. Shall we get going?"

"Sounds good to me," Jeff said. "See you guys there?"

I nodded. "See you there."

Amy climbed into Jeff's truck with him, and Sara and I walked to her Camry. I sat in the passenger seat as we drove across town to Ed Walker's Drive In.

We pulled into the parking lot only a few moments behind Jeff. We all gathered together, went inside, and talked and laughed until our food and drinks arrived. Before we started eating, I held my up my beer.

"Here's to you guys," I said to Jeff and Amy. "Congratulations on your engagement."

****

After dinner, Sara and I said our goodbyes to Jeff and Amy, then drove across town to our next appointment for the evening.

As we walked into the auditorium, most of the crowd had already taken their seats, but a handful of people were still milling about and finding their way in. I scanned the crowd from behind and saw the familiar hat that I was looking for. I got Sara's attention with a tap on the elbow and pointed.

"Over there," I said.

We weaved through the aisles until we reached Natalie and Amelia. They both smiled when they saw us.

"Hey guys," said Amelia. "We saved you some seats."

She stood and gave each of us a hug, although I could tell it took some effort to do so. Even though things were going well, she was still physically exhausted much of the time, but she was looking better each time we saw her. Her hair had already started growing back, but she was keeping it cut short until it completely filled in. In the meantime, she still wore the same hat, which I often referred to as her oversized *yarmulke*.

After the episode with Dr. Carver and the recommendation to add Amelia to the trial, Sara had fought hard to actually make it happen. She had constantly contacted and, dare I say, harassed the poor folks running the trial to include Amelia and, in less than a week, she had worn them down.

Amelia had spent the next five months in Tulsa, going in for daily treatments. Trevor had spent much of that time there with her while school was out, but once it started back up, he stayed with Natalie throughout the week while spending weekends with his mom.

Only three weeks prior, the trial had ended, and

Amelia had moved back home. She was officially in remission.

Sara took the seat next to Amelia and they hooked their arms together.

"I'm so nervous," said Amelia.

"Relax," Sara said. "He'll be great."

The lights dimmed and the chatter in the room died down. The principle appeared on stage, thanked everyone for coming, and introduced the Fourth-grade teacher that had organized the play. Soon after, the show started and Natalie, Amelia and Sara all fidgeted nervously and made quiet, high pitched noises.

I was relaxed. I knew Trevor was going to be great. I had, after all, given him some pointers on acting.

When Trevor's scene finally arrived, there was more fidgeting and whispering.

"Oh my God, he looks so cute," I heard Sara say.

To me, he looked ridiculous, dressed as a milk cow, but I couldn't help but smile. When it came time for his line, I could sense the nervousness emanating from beside me, but Trevor delivered it perfectly.

****

After the play had ended, we milled about in the auditorium, talking with Amelia and Natalie until Trevor came running in and practically crashed into his mother's arms.

"Did you see me?" he asked excitedly.

"I sure did." Amelia leaned down and kissed him. She was suddenly full of energy. "You were amazing. You did so well."

Natalie and Sara threw in compliments of their own as I stood to the side and watched. Finally, Trevor walked over to me.

"Did you see me?" he asked again.

I nodded. "I did."

"Do you think I did okay?"

"Okay?" I asked with an astonished tone. "For a moment there, I thought a real cow had wandered onto the set."

Trevor giggled. I looked around conspiratorially for a moment before motioning him closer. I slipped a Twix bar out of my pocket and covertly handed it to him, where he slid it into his own pocket.

"Good job," I said. He smiled and ran back to his mother.

Chapter 15

Monday, May 26th, 2003
One Year After

I awoke early that morning to the smell of bacon wafting into the guest room. I could hear muted movement coming from somewhere in the house. After getting dressed, I found Sara and her parents sitting at the kitchen table. I quietly fixed a plate for myself and sat down to eat. No one talked much, just the occasional compliment of the food.

When we were finished, Sara and I put on our shoes and left the house, stopping at the end of the driveway.

"Ready?" I asked, as we both stretched.

"Ready when you are," she said.

"Let's go."

We started our run by heading down Commercial, with Sara holding to a leisurely pace for my benefit. Even though we had been running together for the last ten months, I still couldn't keep up with her for very long if she ran at her usual speed. I was, however, getting closer. I felt stronger and better than I had felt in a long time, and I owed it all to a single day that happened exactly a year earlier.

When the river came into sight up ahead, we could see cars filling the lot by the dock and small groups of people were milling about. Rather than continue on, we turned left onto River Road and ran parallel to the park. Sara picked up the pace a bit, and I managed to keep up.

As we neared Highway 64, River Road made a sharp right and joined into Park Road. We took a right onto the loop and slowed to a walk. Up ahead, we could see people gathered around the recently completed memorial honoring the fourteen individuals who had lost their lives in the collapse. Beyond them, in the distance, the I-40 bridge arched up and over the river, once again carrying travelers safely across the muddy waters below.

We exited the road and walked across the grass toward the river. On its gently sloping bank, we took a seat on an old, weathered tree trunk that had washed up in a past flood. We were far enough away that we couldn't hear what was being said as the ceremony dedicating the memorial began.

We watched in silence from where we were. I hadn't wanted to intrude on the gathering, and Sara had agreed. I felt like those who had lost someone in the tragedy deserved to have the moment to themselves. My heart went out to everyone who had lost so much on that day, and I felt a pang of sadness and guilt because I, in turn, had gained so much. It wasn't fair that life could crap all over those who didn't deserve it while lifting up those who did.

Sara must have sensed what I was feeling because she leaned into me and hooked her arm in mine. As it turns out, she had always been very perceptive, I had just never noticed it since I had severely lacked that quality myself.

Sometime later, as people slowly began dispersing, we stood up and turned back the way we had come.

****

When we returned to the Bartlett house, we showered, changed, and said our goodbyes. As I climbed into the passenger seat, my hand feeling slightly crushed, I waved as we pulled out and started our short journey back home.

We took Highway 64 across the river because I had yet to work up the nerve to cross the I-40 bridge. Sara hadn't once made fun of me for it, and for that, and so many other reasons, I loved her.

When the bridge and the river were far behind us, I reached for the radio but had my hand promptly slapped away.

Afterword

On May 26th, 2002, at approximately 7:50 a.m. on a quiet Sunday morning, a barge traveling down the Arkansas River veered off course when its Captain passed out. Before anyone on board realized what was happening, the barge rammed a support that held up a bridge on I-40 near the small town of Webbers Falls, Oklahoma, causing a section to fall away.

The bridge itself arched over the river and, as oncoming traffic crested the apex, they had only moments to react to what they were suddenly seeing in front of them. Traveling at the speed limit of 70 miles per hour, there just wasn't time to stop.

According to witnesses, for the next four or five minutes, three semis and eight passenger cars plunged into the river.

On that same day, a fishing tournament was being held on the river and fishermen in their boats immediately went to assist as best they could. One fired a flare at a semi that was heading for the void. The driver of the semi screeched to a stop and was able to back up and block traffic.

All told, fourteen people from six different states lost their lives in the tragedy.

One year later, a ceremony dedicating a memorial to those who perished took place. Designed by an Oklahoma artist, the memorial uses a section of metal girder from the collapse. The girder angles slightly up and, on the highest end, a statue of a young girl stretches toward the sky in mid-leap, arms raised, releasing a dove. A clock below reflects the time of the collapse. The base of the memorial holds fourteen plaques bearing the names of the victims.

The memorial sits along the banks of the river within the Battle of Webbers Falls Park. In the distance, downstream, the I-40 bridge is visible.

The idea for this book was born one day while driving across the bridge some sixteen years after the tragedy. I wanted to, in the most respectful way possible, remind people what had happened there, and that life is so very valuable and, sometimes, fragile.

I struggled with how to incorporate the very real event into a work of fiction without disrespecting those affected by it. In the end, I decided to keep my distance in an attempt to treat it with the respect and dignity it deserves. I truly hope I did that, but still I worry.

A word about the author...

Kevin Johnson is an avid runner and history buff who was born and raised in the small town of Booneville, Arkansas. He graduated college with a degree in I.T. and now resides in Oklahoma.

Visit him at:

www.kevinjohnsonwriter.com

Thank you for purchasing
this publication of The Wild Rose Press, Inc.

For questions or more information
contact us at
info@thewildrosepress.com.

The Wild Rose Press, Inc.
www.thewildrosepress.com